Riss

MYSTIC PROTECTORS SERIES

BOOK 1

BY

KATHI S. BARTON

World Castle Publishing, LLC

This is a work of fiction. Names, characters, places, and incidents are products of the author's imagination or are used fictitiously and are not to be construed as real. Any resemblance to actual events, locations, organizations, or person, living or dead, is entirely coincidental.

WCP

World Castle Publishing, LLC
Pensacola, Florida

Copyright © Kathi S. Barton 2014
ISBN: 9781629890647
First Edition World Castle Publishing, LLC, February 14, 2014
http://www.worldcastlepublishing.com

Cover: Karen Fuller
Editor: Eric Johnston

Prologue

Michael moved down the hall toward the office. He knew that the other protectors hated to be summoned to this particular office, but he didn't mind. He loved going in and conversing with the creator of all things. Boss, as He wanted everyone to call Him, as it sounded so much friendlier, was a man of men. A kind yet firm man and one who could change things in a beat of a hummingbird's heartbeat. Michael paused in mid-step.

He was going to change things again. Things were running very smoothly right now, and he'd want to shake things up a bit. Michael tried to think what it could possibly be and looked up when someone laughed.

"I was thinking." Boss nodded. "Am I going to regret coming here today?"

"Possibly. And I know you were thinking. I heard. You think much too hard for a man who has it all." Michael snorted, a habit he'd been trying to break himself of. "You think I would lie to you?"

"Nay. I think you believe whatever you wish will be wonderfully simple when it seldom is." Boss moved back into the room He'd come from, and Michael followed. The walls were covered with images of the protectors.

Protectors had long since been the ones who helped Boss in His daily work. A chosen man or woman would be given the assignment to watch over a child when they took their first breath. They never interfered with the person but whispered advice, gave them guidance, and when the time was right, they would be there with them when they drew in their last breath as well.

"I do wish to change things. But not for all of my protectors—just a few." Michael sat down knowing that he'd have to carry out these duties no matter what they were. "You have noticed that they are...unhappy?"

"I have. But it's happened before. They are bored. The last time this happened we gave them a few days to interact on earth and they were happier for it." Boss shook His head. "You do not want that again."

"They wish to leave me." Michael sat there stunned. He'd not heard that. But he knew to leave here would mean— "I don't want that to happen."

"No, nor do I. Who is it? Maybe I can talk to them." Boss shook His head again. "You don't mean to kill them, do you? I know that is the way of things. When a servant is ready to end their time as a protector, they are sentenced to...please tell me of your plan."

"I wish to have them...Perhaps it would be best if I showed you what I have in mind." The wall took another shape and images, a great many of them started to move. And the faster they moved, the more movie-like they became. Twice Michael had asked him to slow down, and after he explained it to him, it moved on. Michael sat there for a long while after the movie stopped and stared at the images of the few men he'd seen there.

"They will not be happy." Michael looked at Boss when He didn't say anything. "Nor will Tholan. He will believe that he is not worthy of such a gift."

"He will be the hardest to convince, yes, but if we deal with him later, then perhaps he will see it is not such a bad thing to have happen to him." Michael doubted that. Tholan had a weight on his heart that no one seemed able to help him with. "I would like to start with these five men before Tholan. I want...do you think you could help me get this started?"

"When would you like for this to happen?" Michael was looking over the files when he realized he'd not been answered. "You have already started this, haven't you?"

"I thought it best that we do some arranging to make sure that the other half of my project was well within hand for us." Boss laughed. "Do not look so crestfallen, Michael. The new group, my Mystics, will be a greater force than we ever imagined."

They worked well into the night, and when Michael left his office, Boss was smiling. He would be, too, if he wasn't so worried about Tholan. The man... Well, that would be something they'd deal with at a later time. But now he had to give the list of men to him and hope that he didn't ask too many questions.

"It is going to be a long time before we will be able to say this worked." Michael heard Boss laugh and flushed. "You should come with me. He will have a fit."

"Nay, he will not. He is a good man. But a man who feels he has failed many. You'll do fine." Boss laughed again. "You are the Archangel Michael, men tremble at the sound of your name."

Chapter 1

Today was a big day. Today his charge was to go into the hospital and finish with her life as she knew it there on earth. Riss was to take her to the holding station where she'd meet him for the first time in person. He was both happy for her and sad; happy that her pain and suffering would end, but saddened by the fact that she'd move on and he'd be assigned another child to watch over until his or her death.

Riss was headed to earth when he felt the Summoning Mist call for him. His first thought was that he was being brought before the judgment panel again. Then he realized he'd been very good the last couple of hundred years and really had nothing to worry about. He turned to the one who'd come for him.

"I need to be with Sadie, it's her final day. I need to be with her to guide her here. Can this not wait until later?"

"No, my lord, you are needed now. I was told to tell you to come posthaste." Riss nodded, thinking how much he disliked the disembodied mists…they were so single-minded. Riss tried to reason with the mist.

"Shall I send another to be with her? She'll be afraid." Again the mist shook his head and Riss had no choice but to follow.

"Someone has been sent." Wanting to argue but holding back, Riss made his way to the upper floors of the offices behind the mist. Someday he was going to stick his hand through one of them to see if they could feel it. He concentrated on this rather than trying to figure out why he'd been summoned on such a day as this.

Riss wasn't thrilled to be there. Things hadn't been the same for him in a very long time, and this was just another thing on his long list. It wasn't as if he hated his job. He actually loved it, but he was tired. And when he was tired, he tended to get himself into trouble. Again. And being called to the upper levels meant he was indeed in trouble again. Riss wasn't a typical guardian. He was one of the ones that would argue when something just didn't set right. Smiling, he realized he loved that part of his job most of all.

Riss had been a guardian for as long as there had been humans to watch over. He supposed he should feel honored to be the one to watch over and guide a human to their afterlife. But if he was honest with himself—and really, he had no choice in that area—he had been thinking of quitting...a drastic move for one such as himself. Thousands of years of watching babies grow up and experience things he never would, only to see them eventually die, was taking its toll on him...a few of his brethren as well.

The doors slid open as soon as he came to the one he'd been called to. Tholan, direct supervisor and his good friend, stood up, but he did not look happy.

"If you pop an attitude with me, I'm not going to be happy. Talking to you right now is not on my top fifteen list. There are too many issues right now for me to have to argue with you." It was a fib, and they both knew it. Tholan lived to argue almost as much as Riss did, and Riss was really good at baiting him into one but wasn't in the mood as Tholan continued. "Please have a seat, and I'll tell you why you were sent for. Oh, and I sent Levi to be with your charge. She's in good hands."

"But not mine." Tholan nodded but didn't say anything. "It's cop an attitude, not pop, and it's top ten, not fifteen. You need to interact more with humans. They're fun. Most of the time. And when they're not...well, then they're not. Sorry, so why am I here? You have to give me my month before you give me another assignment. I'm too tired, and I need it."

"We're changing things. It just came down to me this morning. You're the first I'm telling about it. "Riss stilled. While he was okay with changes, Tholan's tone didn't make Riss think it was a good one. While a thousand and one things ran through his mind, Tholan answered a call from someone.

Change. What could be so monumental that he'd be pulled from his assignment on the last day to be told about it? Were they going to demote him? He had no idea why that popped into his head, but he hoped not. The thought of being an animal watcher again made his skin crawl. They were okay for a few weeks, but for the most part, they didn't interact like humans did. And they didn't make him smile. He thought maybe he'd rather be assigned to a desk than be an animal watcher. Anything was better than watching a—

"Riss?" Riss looked at him, feeling the world crash down upon him. "It's not nearly as bad as what's going through your mind right now. Trust me."

"I'd rather be assigned desk duty than animal watcher. The last time I did that...well over half my life ago...I had a worm. A single worm. They live for years and do nothing but dig and poop. No, whatever it is, I don't want it. Put me in receiving. I'll inventory feathers if you want, but please don't give me another worm. Or better yet, I wish to quit. Now." Riss flushed when Tholan laughed. "You've been at a desk your entire time here, haven't you? You can't imagine what it's like serving animals."

"The Boss has decided to make it so we are not with a single human from birth to death. He's found out that it's as hard on us as it is Him. And we're not connected like He is." Riss doubted that was true but kept his mouth shut. "You, Agon, and Valyn will be the first to take this new system. Sort of help us work out the bugs. As it stands now, you'll each stay with a group we've handpicked for this project and stay with them for a period of no more than ninety days before you'll go to one more in the group of humans. Each of you will rotate in an order that has been handed down to me. We're hoping...well, they are hoping...that over the long run, you'll attach less emotion to a single person."

"No, we'll be attached to several of them at once. I don't want to work out bugs. This is a stupid idea." Tholan raised a brow at him. "Well it is. I'm not cut out to take on more than one person at a time. Having to live a lifetime with one person is hard enough, but taking on several at a time is too much. You have to let me end this now."

"It's a done deal, Riss. You start next week." Riss sat there for several seconds before he got up. "Sit down, I need to give you details."

"I can't do details right now. I have to...I'll come back, but right now I have to get out of here. Give me...please give me a few days. I need to have this." Tholan nodded, and Riss left the office.

Riss was in his room when he realized he was going to have to do this and no amount of trying to think otherwise was going to work. To have to spread himself around like this was going to take its toll on him, and he was so afraid of what would happen. Riss knew he was close to the edge now, and he didn't want to end things that way. He was already stressed out, and this wasn't going to be helpful. Lying on his bed, he looked up at the ceiling and thought of his life as a protector.

Michael had picked him for the job so long ago that now he often wondered if it had been real. But the tattoo, the seal of Michael, was there on his arm for anyone to see. Up until recently he'd worn it proudly. Now…now he just wanted to rest.

"You've never expressed such a desire before." Riss didn't bother looking for the man who spoke. He wasn't really in the room with him but always in the back of his mind. Michael was his good friend too. So many were.

"I've never been this burnt out before. When was the last time you were on earth? Things have gotten insane there." Riss rolled to his side to look out the window as he continued. *"When I was there the other day, five children were killed in an automobile accident that also injured two adults. Things move entirely too fast for us. We've no way to control things."*

"Stop your whining." Riss smiled when Michael snapped at him. He said that to him every few weeks just to get a rise out of him. *"You should have to work with me. One day and I'd bet you'd beg to be put back on protector duty. My job sucks too."*

Riss waited before saying anything more. He had been thinking about this for a while now and wanted to bounce it off someone else because Tholan had ignored him so soundly. Finding someone he could talk to that wouldn't condemn him was hard.

"*I want to quit.*" Riss got up and moved to the large window in his room. It was one of the perks of being so old. He got to have one of the best rooms with the most gorgeous views. His view right now was of earth in the winter. The snow falling on a large open field was beautiful. "*I tried my best to tell Tholan that I really wish to turn in my wings. Then I want to finish my year that I'll have left on earth to die.*"

"*Please don't do that. Maybe we can work something else out. Is this because of the changes that are being made? I think that they'll help you. You'll not have to be with someone for their entire life. You can see many stages of life for a good deal more people at once.*"

"*And see them all die instead of one every few decades.*" Riss opened his outside door and stepped out into the falling snow. It crunched under his feet, and the flakes landed on his face only to melt into tear-like drops. "*No, I've thought about this before I was told today. I've been feeling this way for many years, more than I should.*"

"*Let me talk to someone. I don't want to lose you. You're my best protector.*" Riss snorted, a habit he'd picked up years ago from Sadie. His heart hurt for her too, and that he'd not been there to bring her home. When Michael appeared before him, Riss wasn't really surprised. And when he sat down on the snow-covered bench, Riss sat beside him.

"You're serious about this?" Riss looked at him when he asked. Was he? Yes, he was, more so than he'd been about a great many things.

"I am. I know that once I turn in my wings, I'll only have a year in which to get my affairs in order, but there is nothing really that I have. I've never had the desire to have a home on earth, never owned anything remotely human before, and when my charges come over, I've rarely taken anything that I've thought of to remember them by. I have enough memories as it is." Riss looked at Michael. "I'm tired."

"Then I will make some enquires. Let me have a few weeks to get things working, and once I do, then you may talk to Tholan with me." Michael put out his hand, and Riss stared at it for long moments. "You must take it, Riss. We have struck a deal."

Riss looked at him then. "You'll not put me off then? You'll honestly look into this for me? I think now that I've said it aloud I want it more than ever."

"I will. You have my word that I will make arrangements to have your life as a protector ended. I will do this, to you I swear it." Riss took his hand and felt the power of it go through him. Michael was one of the most powerful beings he knew and could kill a lesser man with just a touch. Riss thought he'd miss him the most of all the people he knew.

~~~

Tholan watched the exchange between the two men. His heart hurt for them both. Riss, because the man was really going to do this, and for Michael, because he hated to lose anyone close to him. Tholan looked at their boss, who stood next to him, and wondered what He would do now. They'd been watching Riss and Michael together since Michael had called them into the conversation.

"He'll be greatly missed." Tholan felt his world shift. He hadn't expected that the man would agree to Riss leaving. But this man was the lord of all of them, and His word would never be challenged. "I will talk with Michael. We'll give him a sendoff he will appreciate, I think."

"You're going to take his resignation then?" He nodded at Tholan. "He's my friend, and he's been with you since the beginning. I think...I don't want him to die. We cannot afford to lose men like him. Yes, he has his problems, but for the most part he's the best we have in the field. Perhaps we could give him something that would—"

"And you're going to question me?" Tholan felt the thunder of His words and lowered his head. "I know what I'm doing, Tholan, and I know what a good friend Riss is to many. What I do not know is why he has not spoken to the others about this. Mayhap they could have helped him. Did you know that he was so tired?"

"No, sir. I did not. He only said something to me today when I tried to talk to him about the changes that you'd made. I felt he wasn't serious. Apparently I was incorrect. Riss was most upset with the changes, but not enough, I thought, to quit us. I had no idea that he was contemplating this as well, to die." He nodded, and Tholan continued. "I should like to speak to him if possible."

"Nay, there will be no need. I will handle this with Michael. If we see fit, I'll let you know what our decisions will be. He may come to you. Then you could speak to him, but do not tell him we have talked. I'd be very happy if you would keep him in the rotations as well. Riss may decide to change his mind." Tholan nodded again and knew that the conversation was over. The room was dimmer by many degrees, and he didn't feel the warmth of Him any longer. Tholan was alone once again

Watching Riss sit in the snow as it covered the tracks that had been, he wondered what would be said if he told them he, too, was burnt out. Tholan only stayed because he knew that he was needed. But his joy for the job had gone away some time ago. He went back to his desk to set up the rotation. Writing Riss's name across the schedule hurt him. Tholan knew that before this decade was finished, he'd be finding someone to replace his good friend.

The changes that had been handed down were mandatory. Four of the older protectors were to rotate around with several different humans over the course of their lifetime. Once one of the humans died, another would be added in to take their place. Some of the men that were in this project had been a watcher for decades to these people. But now they'd share the burden with their friends. Tholan looked at the schedule and wondered about them all.

Tholan had argued that there would be things missed. Humans needed to be cared for twenty-four/seven. Like Riss had said, the world was moving at a much faster speed than when they'd started this, and there were a great deal more humans too.

Tholan looked at his computer. There were thousands upon thousands of names in the roster, and even more humans to watch over. It was small wonder that his men were being burnt out. Riss wasn't the first who had decided to end it all. He was just the first to be a good friend to him. Tholan got up to look out his own window.

"What am I to do?" No one was there to answer him, so he continued to vent his heart. "I fear there will be more and more to leave the services. And when they do, who will watch over them? Who will guide them to the other life, the one that brings them to us?"

No one. Closing his eyes, he thought of his own days as a protector. Few knew that Tholan had spent the better part of his younger days as a protector, and fewer still knew why he was now behind a desk and not out in the world. He had failed. Or so he'd told himself so often that he was the only one that truly believed. Though, now that he thought on it, he was the only one that felt he'd failed at all.

"I failed my charge because I was an arrogant idiot and I couldn't finish my job. I should have done my job instead of hiding out as I'd done. I should have told her what I'd done to her. I should have been killed for hurting her so badly." Tholan felt the hurt of what he'd done, and a tear escaped as he thought about it.

He had gone to his human and was watching her. But she'd fallen, something that happened from time to time, and he went to help her steady herself. But she'd been dead. Fifty-one years before her time. Tholan, in a panic, had lifted her into his arms and carried her to the holding station before the medics were to arrive. But when he arrived, she was not allowed entrance. He'd taken her too soon.

"You'll need to tell her." Michael hadn't been mad then, but he had gotten so when Tholan refused to tell his charge that he'd failed her. "Tell her that she can go back, but it will not be the same. She'll be unable to dance and sing as she'd done before, but she will live out the rest of her days."

Tholan hadn't been able to do it. And when someone else had had to come in to do what he couldn't, he was demoted almost immediately and put to watch over the animals. It was decades before he was able to bid on the position that he had now. But he still thought of her.

Sitting back down at his desk, he finished up his rotation until nearly midnight and stood to leave. When he looked up from his desk, he saw Riss there.

10

He started to ask him how long he'd been waiting when Riss spoke.

"I've talked to Michael. He is going to see about getting me released from my duties." Tholan sat down after offering a chair to Riss as he continued. "I'm supposed to be in the rotation of this plan until he gets back to me. Michael said it won't be long."

"You really are going to leave here?" Riss nodded. "I don't know what to say to you. There are no words to convey how much I'll miss you."

"They'll end my life." Tholan felt his heart ache for the man and nodded. "I will have enough time to put things in my life to rest. Then I will die. I came here to ask a favor of you."

"Anything."

Riss got up to pace. Tholan would do whatever he wanted, even end his life before the allotted time if that's what he needed.

"I would ask that you take my belongings and distribute them to my fellow protectors. I've no one to leave them to." Tholan started to shake his head, but Riss continued talking. "I have my pay as well. A good deal of it. I've never...I know that some of the others have purchased homes and things on earth, but I'd never seen the need. Would you please see that some children's charity gets it?"

Tholan nodded. "Anything else?" Riss just moved back and forth on the carpet. Just as Tholan was going to repeat his question, Riss turned to him.

"I would ask that you go to earth for me. I've...there is one human thing that I've gotten that I've never told anyone of. It's a plot. A place to be buried. I know that you'll not be able to take my body, but I ask that you bury this in the place I have set aside."

He laid a ring on the desk before he continued pacing. Tholan picked it up and looked at it. It was old, probably as old as Riss was. When he started to ask him where it had come from, he saw the inscription.

"Your first charge." Riss nodded. "I had heard that you'd taken something from her, but I'd never thought it to be true. She should have been buried with this."

"She gave it to me. Or who she thought was looking over her. I think from the very beginning she knew someone was there. At times I would hear her speaking, as if to me. I would laugh at her antics, cry when she was brokenhearted, and died a little when she did. I would like this to take the place of my body."

Tholan nodded and put the ring on his desk to put in the safe for later. They talked for a little while longer, and then Riss said he was going to rest. The man looked like he'd been run over several times and left for dead. Tholan thought he'd already given up.

Chapter 2

Kala Marrow sat at her desk for ten minutes just staring at the screen. Terminated. And not even in person. She'd gotten the email first thing when she sat down. And now...well, now she had to gather her things by ten o'clock and put them in a box that had been sitting on her chair with her name on it when she'd arrived today. The letter had also told her not to try to take anything that belonged to the company, for they would be inspecting her *leavings* when she did.

"They're not leavings. That's shit, not my personal belongings." She looked around when she realized she'd spoken out loud and started to sort through her things. There was a lot, too. When they spent ten years on a job, a person could collect a lot of "leavings." Laughing a little, she thought it better than crying. When her friend Dan Carey came by her desk, she tried to ignore him, but he lifted her chin up to see her face.

"I got one too." She glanced at her computer, then back at him. "Today. I have until nine forty-five to get my things gathered up and ready to be inspected."

"Leavings?" He nodded and pulled a chair from another cubical to where she was sitting. "They told me to work until my time was up. Like I'd be able to help a customer get his remote lined up with his television for this company knowing that I'd never get another check from them."

"Yeah, mine said that too. Must be a form letter." He looked around her area and leaned in closer. "I've heard that all but three from this department alone are going to leave today. What do you suppose they'll do about keeping people's cable running if we're all gone?"

Kala had heard rumors that the company was hurting. Just last week she'd had to argue with the accounting department about her check. It had been shorted nearly fourteen hundred dollars in commissions. And the paycheck before that she'd not gotten her attendance bonus. She was glad now that she'd had them pay her now instead of waiting until her next check. That was going to help her for the coming months.

"Do you think we'll get unemployment?" She shrugged. While she was glad it was there to use, she hoped to have another job before it became necessary to get her first check. Kala's goal was to be as independent as possible. Never again was she going to be dependent on welfare and government help.

"I have some money saved. Do you?" Dan shook his head. She didn't think he would. His manner, of course, was to get it and spend it. She supposed that worked if you were thirty-six and still lived at home. But she hadn't lived with anyone for all her adult life, and had lived in an orphanage up until then.

"I have some things lined up. And then we're going to get unemployment. They termed us. We didn't quit." He leaned back in his chair. "I guess you'll go job hunting tomorrow?"

She would, and today after she left there. Things needed to be paid, and they wouldn't be if she didn't have a job. Thinking about what she'd do, she started putting her things into a box that was entirely too small for what she had to stuff in it. She was pulling her pictures off the wall when Dan spoke again.

"I want you to know that I still want us to be friends when this is over." She nodded, thinking that while they were work friends, they'd never done anything outside the job. "Kala, do you suppose they'll cut off our free cable and Internet, too? I hope not. I really like watching television, and so does Momma."

"I would guess they've already done that." She thought about the little postscript at the end of the email. "Did you see where we'd be able to set up our billing for it? I think it said something about two hundred dollars a month for the package we have now. I guess I'll be watching regular television from now on."

She'd never watched much in the first place. It's not that she didn't enjoy what she did glance at, but there really wasn't a great deal of free time in her life. If there was an open slot on the schedule, she usually worked it. And more often than not, she would stay over her shift if someone was running late. Kala had raked up a great deal of overtime that way, and fat commission's checks too.

"I'm not going to be able to watch my shows if they stop it now. I have my DVRs set up to record seven shows just tonight." Kala looked at Dan and frowned. He had that much time to watch seven shows? But then he rarely worked a forty-hour week. She supposed he'd have all kinds of time. Shaking her head, she continued putting her things in the box.

When he was called to his desk by security, she finished getting her things gathered together. By the time she was finished, she had filled a second box and put a few things in her purse as well. When Dale with security came for her, she asked him if he could help her and he nodded, taking the heavier of the boxes.

"I'm sorry this is happening to you, Kala. I thought they were just trimming out the lazy ones. We down there in the hot box never believed it would be you." She felt tears well in her eyes and nodded at him. "We've all been waiting for us to get the axe too, but we found out yesterday that we actually work for the building as of last year. Nobody ever told us."

"You're secure then? That's wonderful news." Kala hugged him as best she could. She really was happy that he'd be working. The man had five kids and a wife to care for. "Did you get to keep everything when they changed you over?"

"Yeah, we got to keep our 401K, too, which surprised us all a little. I've been putting into that thing since you told me to." She nodded, forgetting about her money she'd put in it. She didn't want to ever touch it, but it was something she could fall back on. "My accountant friend told me that not many companies vest you anymore one hundred percent."

She knew that too, and she'd put the maximum amount she could in her account every paycheck. Kala would have to find a way to roll it over without penalties, but she didn't think it would be today.

"Do you know of any places that are hiring?" He told her no, and he didn't mention her unemployment. They'd been friends since she'd been working there her first day, and he would know that she wouldn't take it unless she had to. "I need to hit the streets before anyone else does. I guess they let go of a lot of people."

"They did, but I'm telling you right now, I don't think you have to worry about them others looking for work this fast. Most of them will suck the unemployment out until the very end." She had figured on that as well. "I gotta look through your stuff, honey."

After he went through her things thoroughly, she was out the door. Dale even helped her put her things into her car and gave her a huge hug. Getting in before she made a fool of herself, she handed him her parking ticket and drove off. Kala was sobbing by the time she made it to her little apartment.

It was so quiet in the place that she turned on the television, and when she saw that her cable had already been cut off, she sat down and cried. It was all she could do not to scream out her frustrations. Lying down on the sofa with the television full of static, she closed her eyes. Kala told herself that in a few minutes she'd get up and make herself presentable, but right now her head was pounding and she needed to get rid of it before job hunting. In a few minutes she was drifting off into a restless sleep.

The dream started off strangely. She was in a really bright room with several chairs. It took her several moments to notice the man sitting at the head of the table. When he nodded for her to sit, she did but kept her mouth closed. There was no telling what this dream was, and she didn't want any monsters to come out and eat her, thank you very much.

"You think I'm a monster?" Startled, she shook her head at him. "But you do not believe that I'm real, do you? I assure you that I'm very real, Kala."

"I think you're a dream brought on by too much stress. I've lost my job today." He nodded. Of course he'd know, it was her dream after all. "Where am I?"

"Here, with me." She frowned at him, but before she could get him to clarify what he meant, he continued. "I should like a word with you. It is about your future."

"Of course it is. But I'm not going to take a handout. I've got my pride, you know." He smiled and nodded. "Do you have a job opening for me?"

"I do as a matter of fact. One that only you can do for us." Suddenly, a file was in front of her. "I've made some changes here, and some of the men are not happy with them. I would like for you to help me with one such man."

She opened the file and looked at the blank pages before looking back at him. "And how do I help this man? I'm not going to be his sex-retary. I have my pride too."

"Oh no, nothing like that. Though I must say you'll eventually want to have him in your bed. I'm to understand he's never experienced it before. Sex I mean." She snorted. "He does that as well, though when he does, he does it quietly."

"I'm not here to impress you. I...actually, I have no idea why I'm here. You're saying that I can help this man and will want him to fuck me, but I don't think that's all of it, is it?"

"No. And I would say you're a good deal smarter than I was first told." He leaned back in his chair and regarded her. Kala just watched him. She had no idea what was going through his mind and thought that odd since it was her dream. "What if I told you that you're the first of many such female humans?"

"I would say that you're nuts. Last I knew there were all kinds of female humans in the world. A good deal of them older than me." She leaned forward, resting her hands on the table. "I've never been one to beat about the bush, as it were. Tell me what it is you want."

He stared at her for a full minute before throwing back his head and laughing. "I do not intimidate you at all, do I? Well then, we'll get to it. I'm sending you such a man that you'll never see any like him again. But I think I'll wait a while before you actually see him. I don't want him to know that we've been changing his life around."

"I don't have a job." He nodded at her. "Well, if you think I'm going to provide for him, this guy that I can't see, then you're going to be shit out of luck. I'm going to be broke soon if I don't find something."

"You'll be fine." Kala had her doubts. She was having a dream that she seemed to have no control over. "You like having control over yourself, don't you?"

"Who doesn't?" She looked at the open file again and saw that there was something sort of fading in. She picked it up to look closer at it and found it gave her a slight head pain. Putting it down, she looked at the man. "What is this supposed to say?"

"You can read it once you agree to my terms." She asked him just what they were. "I'll give them to you when you're more ready to understand them. But I will ask that you keep an open mind."

"This is a dream. I'm pretty sure that I'm about as open as I can get here." He didn't say anything, and she glanced down at the file again. This time she could see a word: "Riss."

"You still think you're dreaming?" She nodded. "Then I would suggest that you wake up. There is someone at your door."

Kala sat up, startled. She sat on her couch for several seconds trying to get both her breathing and heart rate under control. But the pounding in her head just wouldn't stop. It took her several more seconds to realize that someone was at the door. Getting up, she looked in the peephole and stared at the man standing there. She opened the door.

~~~

Michael looked at the woman standing in front of him and felt his eyes widen. Goodness, she was a beautiful woman. He started to tell her why he was there when she smiled at him. Michael knew then that this was the right choice for Riss.

"I've been sent to give you your severance pay." She reached for the envelope in his hand and he almost forgot to touch her. It was important for him to keep tabs on her now, and touching her would make that connection. "You'll have to sign for it, I'm afraid."

"Not until I look at it, if you don't mind. I don't want to sign for something that is wrong. I'm sure you understand." He nodded. Michael had been given this just a few minutes ago and was told that she had to accept it. If she didn't then all was lost. She was being helped by his kind to make this work. Riss needed her.

"Why are they getting this to me so quickly? I thought it would take them months." Michael nodded. The truth was, Kala, like so many others at the cable company, were going to get nothing. Even her retirement fund had been pillaged by them. "They cashed out my 401K?"

Michael had no idea what she was talking about until she held up her check. All he'd been told was to touch her, give her the envelope, and to get out. But she motioned for him to come inside, and he had to decline. Riss could not know anyone had been there.

"I don't know, miss. I was told to bring that to you." She nodded and sat down. "Will you be all right?"

"I guess." She looked at him with such sadness that he wanted to comfort her. "I don't suppose you know if anyone is hiring where you work, are they? I just lost my job."

"I will have to check." She nodded and stood up. When she came back with a five-dollar bill he told her he could not take it. "It is against our company policy."

"Please take it. You don't have to tell anyone. You've given me the best possible news today in the form of money. Please let me show you how grateful I am." He nodded and took the money, then simply put it back into her purse without her knowledge. With his magic, he was able to see that the five-dollar bill she'd given him was all the cash she had. It saddened him to think of how much she'd suffered recently and would in the very near future.

Michael left her a few minutes later after making sure she was going to be all right. She had gone through all the emotions that a human could possibly go through, and yet she'd never been angry at him. When she'd cried, he had to leave her. Waiting for the elevator to come, he reached for his boss.

"I have given her the money. I believe she will use it wisely." He agreed that she would as well. *"When will we have Riss see her? I'm hoping soon. I believe it will do them both a great deal of good to be together."*

"He will need to wait until she needs him again. I hate to say this, but as you know, something more in her life happens soon and she will be in a place where he can help her the most. She has to need his strength, and right now she doesn't." Michael stepped into the yawning doorway and moved to his own realm. His boss was waiting for him. "You have her touch, then?"

Michael put out his hand and He took it. There was a look of pure joy on His face and he smiled at Him. "It was enough?"

"It was. She is a hellion I think. Very set in her mind how things should go. I will enjoy watching the two of them figure this out." Michael nodded. "You do not approve, do you?"

"I'm not sure. Riss is a wonderful man, and I enjoy his company a great deal. But will this make more of our kind wish to quit us?" Boss, what everyone here called the man in charge, shook his head. "How can you be so sure?"

"Everyone who sees Riss loves him. He has his troubles. What man does not? He is playful when need be, and serious as well. All who will be privileged to know about this will wish him well. The rest...." Boss shrugged and turned toward His office. "You will watch over her until she is ready for him."

"Of course. I'm on my way to see Tholan now to put her on the list." Nodding to him, Boss sat in His chair. "How much will he need to know?"

"Nothing of what we've done. Tholan is a good man and a very faithful one. He will not question what you tell him." Michael wasn't so sure about that but said nothing. "Tell him to add her to the roster, but have Arryn watch her first. After a time, Riss will come to her. Make sure that you keep an eye on her on the seventh. Riss should be with her then, but make sure if he is not, then you are."

Michael nodded and went to see Tholan. He was sitting at his desk where he always was, but this time instead of burying his head in the computer, he was staring out the window again. Michael had a feeling that Tholan was no happier with his job then Riss and a few others were. It saddened him very much.

"I have a name that I'd like rotated in to the new schedule." Tholan looked at him blankly for several seconds before nodding. "Her name is Kala Marrow, and she is to be with Arryn first, then the rest of the rotation."

"She is how old?" Michael told him she was twenty-seven. "I'll put her in starting tomorrow. I've decided to rotate them every sixty days, then work up to the ninety. That way they will have just enough time to help but not grow overly fond of them."

"You do not approve of this, do you, Tholan?" When he started to protest, Michael held up his hand. "It's all right that you don't. It means that you'll work twice as hard to make it work because you think it will fail. There is a reason for all we do, and there is one for this. Have faith in us."

"I have faith, but this will be harder on them than simply helping one person. We have nine of them now with Miss Marrow, and each of these humans will die before someone will be added in. What will they do if several are to go at once? We have four on this list now that are around the same age."

Michael knew that it would indeed happen. He alone, besides Boss, knew the dates when the humans would die. It was decided the day they were born. Their entire lives were mapped out and kept secret until such time that their protector would need to help them cross over. But he couldn't share this with anyone. It just wasn't done. After making sure that Kala was added to the list, he and Tholan parted ways. He knew the man was frustrated, but there was little he could do about it now.

Going back to his office, he detoured to see if he could speak to Riss again. When he neared his door, he was stopped by Galin. This man made Michael laugh more than anyone he knew.

"Did you know that there is a joke about the chicken crossing the road? And another about who came first, it or the egg? Who cares if the chicken has an unhealthy compulsion to get across the street, I ask you? And why do humans have such an obsession with chickens? There are chicken wings that they eat, as well as any number of sandwiches and restaurants devoted solely to the consumption of them." Galin shook his head, leaning close to whisper. "I do believe at one time someone actually deviled them."

Michael stared at him, confused. "Why on earth would you start a conversation like that? Do you have nothing better to do with your time than to think up things such as this?"

"Nope." Michael felt his laughter burble up. "I do believe that you needed a laugh, my good friend, and what better way to have it happen than to talk about chickens? Oh, and in the event you're wondering, the chicken came first, there are a great many reasons why he crossed the road, and for the record, I love deviled eggs."

Michael laughed, which Galin was correct about…he did need it. "When will you grow up? I'm not sure you should ever be released on the unsuspecting humans. I do believe you're going to be something of an oddity to them."

"Actually, I'm quite tame in comparison." He glanced at Riss's door before he continued. "I've just been to see Riss. He is not home. I heard that he's gone to earth for a few days, something about him seeing the exhibition at the green house in Columbus, Ohio."

Michael nodded and walked down the hall beside Galin. "I guess you've heard about the new rotation?

It's said to make it so that one protector is no longer responsible for the life of a single human."

"I have. Not sure how that will lessen our pain, but I'm not in it, so I'm not worrying." Michael knew that he would be before it was ended. "Do you suppose that's why Riss has been so standoffish? That he is in the rotation?"

"I believe so." Michael sat at the table in the cafeteria and was brought a glass of water, as well as a bagel with creamed cheese. "He will be sharing the burdens of others. It will help somewhat, I think."

"Doubtful. It hurts a great deal, as you know, to have to bring one over. I'm not looking forward to my charge leaving. He's been a real hoot." Michael nodded, not sure what "hoot" really meant.

After a nice breakfast full of good food and company, he and Galin parted ways. In four days, his charge would be coming to them, and then Galin would have his month to rest. After that, he, too, would be put into the rotation. Michael just hoped this was a good idea.

Chapter 3

"I don't understand." She looked at the paper again. "This says that you've given me notice prior to this. I've never received anything."

"Be that as it may, miss, you have fifteen days to get out of the building before the construction starts." The man took the sheet of paper back and showed her where to sign. Riss wanted to go to her, the need to comfort so strong. He moved closer to her and leaned into her small frame. He could smell her perfume.

"I've never...where am I supposed to go?" The man shrugged at her, and Riss found the sudden urge to hit him. The feeling had never entered his body before, and he actually kind of liked it. But he looked at Kala again, and his heart ached.

After the man left her, she went into the kitchenette to sit down. Riss went with her and stood watching her. He could feel her sorrow and pain and wanted very much to help her. Thinking about what Arryn had told him about her so far, he wondered how much more the poor girl could take and moved closer to talk to her.

He really didn't *talk* to her as much as encourage her. Just whispering in her ear to have faith and to keep her chin up had worked so well for him before with humans. Riss leaned close to her and sniffed again. Her perfume smelled like his small garden...fresh and warm even in the winter time.

"You'll be fine. Keep your faith and things will improve." Her snort startled him, but he continued. "Things are always looking up."

"Since when?" He took a step back at the anger in her voice. "No matter how hard I try, I keep getting the shit knocked out of me and I have to start all over again. Well, I'm sick to death of it."

He started for her again when she stood up and started pacing. The anger in her body made her rigid and her footsteps firm. Riss was amazed at how beautiful she looked, and wished for the first time in his life that he was a human so he could tell her so.

"There are any number of reasons I should simply take a knife and cut my wrists open. If I wasn't so afraid of the landlord wrapping my body up and tossing it into a dumpster, I'd do it. Why do I have to have this happening to me all the time?" He reached for her and felt her skin beneath his fingers just before she stopped and stared in his direction. "What the fuck was that?"

Taking a step back, Riss was afraid. Not of her, but the sensation that moved throughout his body. He felt...well, hungry came to mind, but he knew it couldn't be that. While he could eat, it was more of a habit than anything else. He felt hunger for her.

"Who's there?" It wasn't the first time a human had asked that of him, but it was the first time he wanted to show himself for one. When she took a step in his direction, he took two back. Riss had no idea why, but he thought if she touched him now, she'd be able to see him.

When she started pacing again, he let out a breath. She started talking almost immediately, but this time he was paying little attention. He needed to talk to someone, but for the life of him wasn't sure who to call. But Michael contacted him first by simply showing up.

"She knows you're here." Riss nodded, not really sure how Michael knew, but then the man seemed to know everything. "Did you let her see you?"

"No." Riss flushed when he realized how loudly he'd spoken. "No. I didn't. Though I'm not sure, but I believe had she touched me, she would have seen me."

"She would have."

Riss waited for him to continue, but when he didn't, Riss looked at Kala. She was still talking to herself, but her words were garbled and he wasn't sure why.

"I have made it so she may vent without you hearing. She is not being very complimentary to you at the moment."

"She does not know me." Michael nodded, and Riss felt a surge of anger toward him. "You know something."

"Yes. I know a great deal. As a matter of fact, I would say my information is countless." Michael grinned before continuing. "You are angry. It's a good feeling on you."

"I don't know what you're talking about. I'm merely upset that I nearly showed myself to a human."

"Would that have been so bad?" Riss looked at Kala, then back at Michael. "What if I told you that if she saw you it would not be the end of the world? You would appear as a human to her, and she would know no difference. You'll be gone from here soon, so what should it matter if she has a glimpse of the man you are?"

"I'm not sure what you mean." But Riss did. He was telling him that he could interact with a human, this human, before he died. "I would prefer to leave my life just as it is. I'm not interested in having a relationship with a human."

"Suit yourself." Michael looked at Kala, and Riss felt another emotion that he'd never had before. Jealousy, white hot jealousy. "Would you like to know what she does with her anger?"

"No." Riss suddenly wanted his friend gone. "I've got things under control now. I don't know what happened with her, but I'm better now."

Michael looked at him, and Riss had the urge to squirm, something he'd never wanted to do in this man's presence. "You may think you do, but you are far from it. Control, I mean."

Riss shifted on his feet and looked at Kala. She was still pacing, but now there were tears. He wished he could hear what she was saying but was afraid she'd still be talking to him. When Michael cleared his throat, he looked at him.

"Arryn will be able to return tomorrow. I can watch over her until he can be here." Riss found himself shaking his head at Michael before he could think what he was doing. "You wish to remain here?"

"I will finish my shift for her today. She will not need you to keep her safe." Looking at Kala again, he continued. "She isn't so hard to watch. And I've nothing else to do until you make your decision as to who I will have next."

"As you wish." When Riss looked again, Michael was gone. Riss watched Kala for a few more seconds as what she was saying became clearer. She was still ranting about how her life was uncertain, and she was simply tired of it. Riss could relate to her feelings, but not in how she wanted to handle things.

"I have two weeks to find a home, pack my stuff, and move. How do I do that? Burn the place down with me in it comes to mind." She sat down, and he watched the tears flow. "I'm such a failure. I've always been something of a flop, and now...who the hell cares?"

She stood up abruptly and moved out of the kitchenette, and Riss followed her. When she was in the bedroom again, he watched as she pulled hanger after hanger out of the tiny closet and tossed them with the clothing on them to the floor. He had no idea what she was about until she left him to go to the bathroom, only to return seconds later with a large trash bag. Watching her stuffing things into the bag with such force as to tear it, Riss sat down.

"You're going to be fine. And you're not a failure. You're brilliant and beautiful." Kala didn't pause in her packing but pushed things harder into the plastic. "I know you don't think so, but I bet in a few months when you're settled in a new job and a new place to live, you'll wonder why you were so upset."

"Shut up." Riss wanted to take her into his arms again, and nearly stood up to do so when she spoke again. "I'm done with this life. I've had enough."

This time when she went into the bathroom, he followed. She was running a bath, and he had a feeling she wasn't going to go into it with the idea to relax. Moving to the front of the tiny apartment, he went out the front door to the hallway beyond. Summoning Michael, he waited for him to show.

"How do I appear to her? She is about to kill herself, and this is all I can think about doing." Michael moved through the door and was gone for longer than

Riss thought necessary. When he returned, he frowned.

"You think of being a human." Riss waited for more, but apparently Michael thought he knew what he was to do next and disappeared. Riss thought of all the things he'd do to the man once he saw him again and thought of Kala in the other room.

Being a human was something he'd never thought of. They were creatures that, while he found fascinating, he was still afraid of. So when he had to concentrate on being one, it was more difficult than he'd thought. Finally, after what he was afraid was too long, he knew that he'd achieved it. Reaching to the bell he'd seen others press, he heard the tinkle of the sound through the door.

~~~

Kala pulled her robe on to go to the door. Whoever was on the other side was going to get an earful when she opened it. Laying on the bell like it was their job, she thought maybe she'd pull the sucker out after she murdered the person pressing the button. When she tore open the door, she nearly swallowed her tongue when she saw him standing there.

"Hi." Kala nodded at his greeting but couldn't for the life of her think how to use her mouth. "I was wondering what you're doing."

Doing? Right now, she was trying her best to figure out why she was having a massive heart attack and how not to drool on the best looking man she'd ever seen. Nodding, she felt at once stupid and needy when he smiled.

"Miss?" He started to step toward her, and Kala had the overwhelming need to step toward him. But instead she stepped back.

"What do you want?" The man stepped back but smiled. Kala had a feeling he was as uncomfortable as she was right now. "I was about to kil...take a bath."

"I see." He put out his hand, and she reached for it without thinking. "I'm Riss. I live around here."

"Kala Marrow." She frowned at him, trying to remember where she'd heard that name before. "Do I know you?"

"I don't think so." He looked down the hall, and she did as well. Dan was coming toward her, but he'd not looked up after getting out of the elevator. Kala didn't want to see him right now. Grabbing Riss by the shirt, she pulled him into her apartment and closed the door quietly behind him. He was staring at her strangely when she put her fingers to her lips to quiet him.

The knock on the other side of the door had her tensing up, but as soon as Riss put his hands on her waist, she felt relaxed. Looking up at him, she realized he had the most beautiful eyes she'd ever seen on a man...or anyone for that matter. They were as clear as glass and seemed to shine back at her. When he leaned toward her she held her breath, knowing that if he touched her more than he was at the moment, she was going to drag him to her bed.

"Do you not want that man to know you are home?" She shook her head and felt Riss's sigh as it fanned over her throat. "I will protect you."

When he leaned back, resting his head on the door, she looked at him again. In that moment, Kala knew that he would do just that too...protect her at all costs. Moving her hands up from his arms to his shoulders, she meant only to shove him away but pulled him closer to her.

"Kala," he breathed her name before she took his mouth. Warm, soft lips met hers, and she ran her tongue over his mouth, hoping...no, needing for him to allow her in. When she felt his mouth open, she dove in with her tongue and moaned at the taste of him. His grip on her waist had her stepping closer to him until she could feel every muscle, every hard plane, and his cock thickening between them.

Kala had never been kissed before. Men had tried, she realized then, but no one had ever done this to her, made her feel, simply feel, like this man currently was. When he rolled her so that her back was against the door, she moaned again and rocked into his groin. When he tore his mouth from hers, Kala whimpered and tried to pull him back.

"I've never felt this way before." She nodded at him, agreeing with him with all her heart. "I want to touch you in ways that I shouldn't. Taste you by biting into your flesh and taking you into me."

"Please." Pulling him to her throat again, he suckled her pounding pulse into his mouth and bit down gently. "Riss, please. I need you."

Her body was on fire for him, every part of her wanted him, and she wasn't sure where to have him start. Nothing like this had ever happened to her. Never had she had such an immediate and profound connection to a person after such a short time. Her need for him to make love to her had her body wet and open for him. And for whatever reason, she knew that he'd be the only one who would be able to quench this overwhelming thing that was between them.

Taking his hand from her waist where he held her so tightly, she moved it to her breast and squeezed his palm over her. His head lifted from her throat, and she watched as he opened her robe slowly.

"I've never done this before." Something in her mind clicked, but it was gone before she could catch it. "Your skin is warm, almost hot, and you taste of winter and heat. I want to lick you in places that should be left for another. I want to...I need to do things to you that I've only just now thought of."

When her breast was exposed, he leaned down and licked the tip. Her nipple felt as if he'd scorched her, and she had to look to see that he hadn't. Pulling him closer again, she nearly cried out when he pulled her hard peak into his mouth and suckled. Then when he opened his mouth over her and took all of her into him, she wrapped her fingers into his hair and held onto him. Crying out when he rocked his hard length into her, Kala felt herself building up to the best orgasm of her entire life, she just knew it. Then someone said her name loudly behind her.

"Kala, I know you're in there. Open up." The pounding on the door had her vibrating, and she moaned when Riss pulled away. "Kala Marrow, what the fuck are you doing? Open this door. I need to talk to you."

"Go away, Dan." But it was too late, she saw. Riss was pulling away from her. When he pulled her robe closed and stared at her, it was all she could do not to beg him to take her right then and there. "Dan, you fucking prick, I hate you right now."

"Let me in." She looked at Riss, who seemed not to just be stepping back from her but putting miles and miles of distance between them. Kala wanted to cry. She needed this man, and if his cock was any indication, he wanted her as well. He looked as if he was as thick as her wrist and at least nine inches long. She wanted to find out right now.

"I said to go away." Riss took another step back from her, and she turned to the door. There was no way she was going to stare at a man who had completely devastated her in such a short amount of time. "I'm busy right now. Come back later. Tomorrow, come back tomorrow. For dinner."

"I need to talk to you. Just open the damned door now." She leaned her head against it and took several deep breaths, hoping that it would wash the scent of Riss from her. Kala barely heard Dan as he begged to be let in now.

"Just come back at six tomorrow. I'll fix dinner and you can tell me what you want." He was quiet for a long while, and she turned to look at the man behind her. He still looked as shell-shocked as she felt, and his cock was as hard as ever. "I think you should leave, too, when he does."

When he nodded, she wanted to beg him to stay. There was something so...so very powerful about this man, and she found she wanted to explore him. Every single inch of him. Dan said he'd be back at six, and she waited until she heard the bell to the elevator sound and the noise that it was moving before she opened the door again. This time she didn't look at Riss, but at the door as she held it.

"I'm truly sorry that I've hurt you." She didn't try denying that he had, nor did she acknowledge that he'd spoken. But when he stopped in the doorway and lifted her chin with his fingers, she had no choice but to look at him. "There is no reason for you to harm yourself. You'll be all right."

It took her several seconds after he was gone to realize what he'd said to her. For whatever reason, he'd known what she'd been about to do. Looking down the hall to tell him to explain himself, she saw that he was gone. Wondering if she'd missed the elevator coming up, she stared at the door when it dinged again that it had returned to her floor. Mrs. Taylor, who lived across from her, nodded as she left the elevator alone and hurried into her own home. Kala closed her door and went to her kitchen. There were strange things going on, and she was too stressed to deal with them.

Kala sat at her table and tried to think about what had just happened. It had to be a dream. There was no way she would have thrown herself at a man, a stranger, so quickly. And the fact that he'd known that she was just seconds away from slicing open her own wrists was simply not possible. More than that, there was no way he could have made her feel so...so...so something in a few seconds. He'd been a dream. A stress-related dream that had her trying to get over the fact that she was going to be homeless in a few days. Looking around the kitchenette, she wondered how the hell she was supposed to get ready for all this in just two weeks. That's when she noticed the feather lying on the floor near the doorway.

Getting up, she moved toward it with trepidation. She had no idea why the sight of something so soft and harmless had her terrified, but it did. When she leaned down to pick it up, she hesitated, trying to think how it had gotten into her house. Lifting it to her nose, she sniffed it and found her body reacting to it as if Riss was still there and touching her. Going back to the kitchenette, she laid it on the table while she got herself a glass of water.

"It's a feather, Kala, you've seen them before." Yeah, she told herself, but not as big as this one was. "So what? It's a big feather. It has nothing to do with the dream you had. It's a fucking feather. Get over it."

But for some reason her head wouldn't let it go. The man with the file, just before she'd left him, he'd stood up, stretched, and he'd had feathers. Actually, he'd had wings, the kind that seemed to be made from large feathers like the one she had. Shivering, she picked up the snowy white feather and took it to her bedroom, where she put it in the drawer. Then she went into the bathroom.

"I have to find a job today and a place to live. Not necessarily in that order, but today." Letting out the water from the now cold bath, she stepped into the spray of hot water. Once she was out of the shower and dressed, she'd told herself that Riss wasn't real and that the feather was from her pillow. A pillow that she had fluffed up when she'd made her bed that felt like it was made from foam. "It's not really. I'm just stressed."

Once out of the apartment, she felt better...more alive, she supposed. By the time she was in her car and moving toward the newspaper office, she'd convinced herself that all of it had been a dream. There was no way she'd nearly had sex with a man in her living room, and the feather was just that. A feather. As she pulled into the side street to get a paper, she felt much better. And when she saw the help wanted pages, she knew this was going to be a good day. Going over each one, she found seven that she could do and four more she'd put on her list to send a resume to. Kala was going to be working by tomorrow. She just knew it.

Chapter 4

Riss was supposed to be with her right now, but all he could think about was what he'd done. He'd not just interacted with a human, but he'd kissed one. And had her naked breast in his hand and mouth. Riss looked up from his table when someone sat down with him. Groaning to himself, he wondered how he could politely ask Arryn to leave him alone.

"I heard you took over the duties for Miss Marrow." Riss frowned. He'd only said he'd finish the day, not take over. "Thanks. The man I have now is sort of funny. I've had a good time with him today."

"I'm not her protector." Riss looked around when he realized he'd shouted again. "I mean, I told Michael that I'd watch her yesterday. I never meant that I'd stay with her."

"You'd better clear that with him then. I'm working with another charge now, and your name is on as her protector." Arryn leaned back in the chair he'd turned to sit on backwards. "She's not like others, is she?"

"What do you mean?" Riss picked up his tray of fruit that he'd not touched and stood up. "I'm going to talk to Michael and get this straightened out."

"I mean she doesn't seem to be the kind that you and I usually watch over. Our charges seem to be quieter, reserved, and more...I don't know. Softer I guess." The thought of how soft her breast had been in his hand and the hard nipple had been in his mouth had Riss sitting down. "She also seems to be a woman who would crumble at the first sign of trouble."

"I didn't see that." Arryn cocked his head and Riss felt he had to continue for some reason. "She's stronger than you think. I heard her arguing with herself just before I left her yesterday, and I think she is made of sterner stuff than most humans."

"How so? I mean the woman has lost her job, and from what I saw in her file, she will be homeless in a few days. The new owners were to bring the eviction papers to her yesterday. It was why I'd agreed to go to the new human, because I knew that you'd be with her when it came." Riss wondered why he'd not been given her file but looked at Arryn when he continued. "She is going to have a hard time finding a place to live, because without a job no one will rent to her. And from what I saw, she doesn't have enough money for a down payment on a home of her own either."

Riss started to say something when he felt something wash over him and had to let go of the tray to grip the table, he felt so unsteady. Getting up when the feeling didn't go away, he staggered to the door and into the hallway ignoring Arryn, who was asking him if he was all right.

He felt...well, it wasn't really ill, but he felt as if he was overheated. More than that, he needed something. Riss felt as if he were on fire and his wings were burning to be set free to wrap around them...no, him, and fix this. He looked up when he realized that Tholan was speaking to him.

"Are you unwell?" Riss shook his head, then nodded. "That is not at all helpful, Riss. Either you are not well or you are well. Which is it? I've a meeting to attend, but I will not leave you like this."

"It's all right. I'll be all right." Riss hoped so as his friend moved down the hallway to the large conference room. Hanging onto the walls as he moved toward his chamber, the feeling of overwhelming need of something came over him again. He wondered briefly if it had anything to do with his missing part...the feather he'd realized was gone when he'd gotten up that morning.

He'd heard from someone once that a missing feather was akin to missing an arm or a leg. Riss hadn't believed that for a second, but right now he wasn't so sure. The only way to settle this was to go back to her home and find it. Once it was back on his wings where it needed to be, he'd be well again. At least he hoped so. The best way to find out was to leave right now.

Before he appeared in her home, Riss had an urge to take a cold shower. He had no idea where that came from, but he was aching so badly that he wanted to try anything. And his cock was hard. Never in all his years had it been so full feeling and painfully hard, not even when he'd been with her the day before. Kala had made him feel this way too. Moving through the portal that took him to Kala's home, he ended up in the kitchen where she'd nearly fallen.

Riss looked everywhere, even in the trash bin where he thought she might have put it when she'd found it. He had no idea where else to look when he realized there were noises from the other room. Not sure what he'd find, Riss made his way to the back of the house, and when he realized that the sounds were coming from her room, he went through the door and hoped he wasn't walking in on her and a lover.

"Oh my." Riss felt his body flush hot again as she lay there naked. Her breasts were full and her nipples as pert as they had been yesterday when he'd taken them into his mouth. As he watched, she cupped one and pinched it hard between her thumb and finger, and Riss felt his mouth water. To taste her again, to suckle such a treat would be wondrous. When he looked down her body, he felt the thickening of his cock make his knees weak, and it was all he could do to stand and watch her. Her womanly parts were there for him to view, and what he saw made him want to free his hard cock and touch her with it.

Looking down her body, he saw that her other hand was busy sliding in and out of her glorious womanhood. Taking a step toward her, he felt as if he'd run several marathons twice, and still, the feeling of need rolled over him. He was at the bottom of her bed before he could think that he should not even be in her room, and even more so, he wanted to join her in the bed. But when he looked at her slick fingers, he moaned, and everything she was doing stilled.

"Come here." He looked behind him and there was no one there. When she sat up on the bed, her breasts swaying to her heavy panting, he realized she could see him again. "I said to come here. I need you to finish me."

"Finish you?" She put her wet fingers into the top of his pants and practically dragged him over the edge. Protesting seemed to be something he should be doing, but all thought of stopping her left his head when she took his mouth.

Her tongue swirled with his, moving in and out of his mouth like her fingers had been over her womanhood. Riss put his hand on her shoulder to push her away, but met with the heavy flesh of her breast. Her moan, loud and full of something he'd never heard before, had him cupping it as he'd seen her doing.

"Please? I need you to make me come." Riss moved his mouth down her throat, tasting her sweat-dewed skin. When her hard peak seemed to beckon him, he pulled it into his mouth and suckled hard. He had no idea what it was like to come, but if this feeling was anything near to what she needed, he would help her. Biting down once had her curling her fingers into his hair, and Riss opened his mouth wider over her and took as much of her creaminess into him. His cock hurt so badly now that he cupped it with his free hand to try to relieve the pressure.

"I want to suck you." He nodded, not really sure how that would work as he had no breasts as she had, but he was willing to try anything right now. When her fingers had his pants open and her hand wrapped around his cock, Riss hissed out his approval and rocked involuntarily into her tight hand. That's when he saw his feather.

There in her hand was his missing part. Before he could ask her for it, she took it to her breast and ran it over her. Riss cried out when he felt it over his own body and rocked harder into her hand. Whatever was going on between them had just gotten more intense, and he didn't want it do stop.

Riss was turned and lying flat on his back when she freed his cock. Embarrassed to be caught in such a state, he reached down to cover himself, but she wrapped her hands around his and they both began to slide up and down his shaft. The feather in her other hand moved over his tip. Again, it was as if they were connected though the part of him that had no business being used as it was. She moved it over her breast, and

Riss threw back his head and moaned. But not seeing her as she moved over him wasn't an option, and he looked down her lovely body.

Kala was soaking his thigh as she rode her body over him. Riss found he wanted to taste her cream. Running his finger though her wet curls, he took it to his mouth and moaned at her taste. If there was anything better than this, he was sure he didn't want to know. Her hand moved up and down him faster now, and he felt his wings tingle and his balls tighten. When she let him go, Riss whimpered, but nearly came up off the bed when she put her mouth to him.

"Oh yes," he cried out over and over. Each time she licked him from root to tip, he felt his eyes cross, and when she took him fully into her mouth and swallowed around him, Riss felt everything in him let go. Crying out, he knew his cock was letting go and his body was spilling into her. When she sat up suddenly, he was sure he had no more, but she wrapped her hand around him again and guided her over his still throbbing cock. When she slid down, taking him deep inside of her, Riss knew a moment of pure bliss.

Kala didn't move for several seconds but sat with him deep inside of her while she looked down at him. When she handed him his feather, Riss did the only thing he could think of and brushed it over her breasts. Her rolling her hips over him had him sitting up and putting his hand to her hip while he played his part of him all over her body.

Her nipples were so pink he wanted to taste them again and again. When he brushed his feather over them, each tiny strain seemed to send a message to his own body, telling him more, it wanted more. Kala put her hand on his shoulders, and Riss rolled over. Being deep inside of her in this position gave him the perfect view of her face when he moved inside of her. Rolling his own hips to mimic her, he knew when he'd touched something inside of her that made her moan loudly, giving her more pleasure than he'd ever felt before. When she wrapped her legs around his waist, locking her ankles behind him, Riss rocked harder and faster into her until the same feeling he'd had before when he'd released began to build again. As soon as she screamed, her body milking his as she did so, Riss pounded deeper until he had his own release. Taking her mouth as he filled her, Riss wondered if he could do this again, move within her wet, hot body over and over until the feelings that he'd just had were to repeat until he couldn't move.

Suddenly his release was upon him again, and he threw back his head and roared out. Never had anything felt so draining and energizing at the same time. Dropping down onto her, Riss tried to catch his breath while his body seemed to feel it had come home.

Riss knew he was heavy, but he couldn't move, and even if he had wanted, it was all he had the strength left to do. Her fingers danced down his back, and Riss wanted to ask her if it was always like this with her, and realized just what they'd done. Lifting his head, he looked at her and tried to think of something profound to say.

"You have my feather." She nodded and grinned, and he felt foolish. "I came back to get it, and you were in here. I never knew such wondrous things could be done with something so small and soft."

"I felt you when I used it on my body. Don't ask me how, but when I found it in my kitchen last night, all I could think about was coming with it next to my skin." She closed her eyes and smiled. "I'm very tired.

You've worn me out completely. I just need a quick nap and we'll talk, okay?"

Riss watched her breaths become even and her body go lax beneath his. Moving as slowly as he could so as not wake her, Riss got up from her bed and smiled. Then he looked at her and realized that he'd done something that he never should have. He'd had sex with a human. What had he done?

Gathering his clothing, he moved back as far from her as he could go. Then when his back touched the wall behind him, he nearly cried out. Yanking on his clothes, Riss tried to think what he was supposed to do now. Moving through the portal again, he went straight to his bedroom and paced.

~~~

Kala woke feeling as if she'd slept for a month. Stretching her arms over her head, she smiled knowing that whatever she'd eaten before she'd gone to bed, she was having it every night. Then she felt the feather that she'd had clutched in her hand touch her cheek. It was then that the entire night came rushing back.

"Riss?" No answer and she got up to see if he was in the bathroom. When she found the room empty, she grabbed her robe and went to the kitchen. No one was there either, and she sat down. "Sex. We had the most incredible sex of my life and he left me."

Kala looked around the room she'd started packing last night, and realized she'd been talking to herself a great deal lately...and answering herself. Standing up, she went to the bedroom to shower and change. Getting under the hot spray, she realized how sore she was and nearly smiled again. Christ love a noodle, she wanted that lovely dream again. And it had to be that. No way would she have had sex with a near stranger and enjoyed it so much. But she knew as surely as she was standing there that he was real and that he'd left her after they'd had sex, left without a word.

Kala had planned to go back out and job hunt again. But yesterday had been a complete bust, and she needed to get herself in a better frame of mind before she could do that again. Not only had she not gotten a job, but no apartment either. The two places she'd looked at within her budget wouldn't even let her put a deposit down because of the fact that she had no job. Fighting tears again, she got out the things to make a pot of chili, just remembering that Dan was coming over soon.

It was simmering on the stove when she'd finished packing up what she could in the kitchen. There really wasn't a great deal that belonged to her. A mixer she'd not used in years, a coffee pot she got as a present one year from someone at work when they'd gotten two of them, and a few dishes. Leaving the latter behind, she went to the living room and stopped in her tracks when she saw Riss standing there.

"You're no longer welcome here." He nodded but didn't move. "How the hell did you get in here anyway? I locked that door."

"I don't need a key. Would you please give me back my feather?" She put her hand over her pocket to protect it from him. For some reason, and she had no idea why the thought popped into her head, she knew if she gave it to him she'd never see him again.

"I don't know what you're talking about." He flushed and she smiled. "You mean the one you used on my body this morning? The one that made me come so hard that I saw stars?"

This time when he flushed, she laughed. There was something very sexy about a man that looked like him being embarrassed. When he put out his hand, all she could think about was how he'd touched her with it, and wanted to ask him if he'd like to use his feather on her again.

"Why do you have a feather, and why does it feel like you're touching me when I move it over my body?" He looked away, then back at her. Riss was hiding something, and she was almost afraid to find out what it was. "Riss? Tell me why a feather would make me feel like you're touching me?"

"It's a part of me." She grabbed the back of the couch she was standing next to. "I'm not supposed to tell you anything. I'm just here to protect you."

"You weren't supposed to fuck me?" He flushed a brighter shade of red before he shook his head. "Why do you have feathers? Are you a chicken? A bird?"

"I'm a protector." Kala waited for him to say more, but he simply stood there for a few seconds. "May I have my feather please? I need it to become whole, and I cannot move on without being whole."

"You mean that this feather you think I have is a part of your body? Like wings?" He nodded, and she felt the earth move under her feet. "Show me."

"I cannot." Kala didn't believe him for a second and started to tell him so when he took a step toward her. "I would very much like to take you back to your bed and do those things to you again, but I was told that I must either decide to stay or leave you. My time has come to an end."

"What time would that be?" He was nearly touching her now and she put her hand to his chest. "I'm not giving you this until you explain yourself to me. And I don't mean these half-truths that you're giving me."

"I want you. I want to have sex with you again. Touch you in ways that make me hard again." She ran her hand down his chest to his cock and cupped her hand around his thickness. "You make me feel things that I should not."

"You can taste me like I did you." She felt him rock into her hand. "Lick me until I come in your mouth like you did mine."

She moaned when he moved her hand and rocked into her pussy. She wanted this man more than she thought possible, and when he kissed her, she spread her legs wider and nearly cried out. Then he moved hard against her clit. If he did it again, she was going to come, but she didn't care. He stepped back from her, and her body burned.

"I cannot." She nodded but started to undress. He was not going to leave her this way. "You must know that I will not have sex with you again. I...I have been...."

Tossing her shirt to the back of the couch, she took off her bra and dropped it to the floor. When she put her hands into the top of her pants to pull them off, he took another step back. She slipped them off with her panties and stood before him naked, with only the feather in her hand.

"If you don't want to watch me, I would suggest that you leave now. Because I'm going to come with or without you." Kala traced the feather over her breasts to her navel and moaned. "Can you feel this, Riss?"

"Yes. All over my body." She closed her eyes and ran the feather over her mound and then over her thigh, teasing herself. When he spoke again, his voice was thick with need, and she felt herself get wetter because of it. "Will you reach a peak this way?"

"Yes. It won't be as satisfying as this morning had been, but I'll come." She looked at him and realized how stiff he was. Taking the feather to her nipple, she danced it over the peak as she slid her fingers into her pussy. Closing her eyes, she told him how she was feeling. "I'm so wet. And my clit is hard, like your cock. Do you want to eat me, Riss?"

He didn't say anything, but she knew that he wanted her as much as she did him. His harsh breathing had her panting, because she could feel how badly he wanted her. When his fingers touched her thighs, she opened her eyes and looked down at him. He had taken off his shirt and pants but left his boxers on. Kala moved her foot up his thigh to his cock and gripped him with her toes.

"You're not going to give it to me, are you?" She moaned when he kissed the area above her pussy. "You've given me very little choice, too, in wanting you. It is forbidden, but you are making me want to break the rules."

"Shut up and put your mouth on me." His chuckle had her wanting to bash his head in, but he slid his tongue down her to her apex. Opening her nether lips, he stared at her for several seconds, and she could feel herself getting wetter and wetter. "Riss, please?"

His mouth moved close to her clit but never touched her where she wanted. She was rocking her hips to get him to take her when he slid his fingers into her sheath that had her scream out his name. And when he finally took her, his mouth nipping at her swollen nub, Kala came so hard she saw stars. But he wasn't finished with her yet.

Over and over he ate at her, bringing her to climax so many times she was weak with them. And when she thought she'd had enough, he'd bring her again.

Finally, she couldn't take it anymore and pulled his head from her.

His face was covered in her juices, and his eyes were dark silver now. She could see his need. He wore it like a mask. Telling him to lay back, she watched him settle to her floor as she knelt before him.

"Do you have any idea what your mouth does to me?" Kissing his nipple, she moaned when he pulled her hand down to his cock. "I'm going to ride you, but first I want to lick my juices off your mouth."

"Your taste is like heaven to me. I could drink from you for the rest of my days." Riss moaned when she pulled the elastic of his boxers over his cock and it caught. "If you touch me, I will erupt. I'm aching."

"Would you like to come in me again, Riss?" He nodded and helped her swing her legs over his hips. "I'm going to make sure you're ready for me. Then I'm going to take you into my pussy and ride your cock until you come."

"I am ready for you. I shouldn't be, but I am." He moaned again when she leaned to his cock after scooting down his legs. "Kala, I should very much like to come in your mouth again. Would that be possible?"

"I want to feel your cock inside of me. I want to feel your thick, hard shaft fucking me." Riss held her head while she licked him from root to tip. Suckling on the tiny eye, she played with him with her tongue until he was begging her to finish him. Sitting up again, she moved up his body, and with her hand at his shaft lowered herself onto him. Stilling, she looked down at him and felt a connection she'd never had with anyone before seem to snap into place.

"You're going to leave me, aren't you?" He nodded and held her hips when she started to move off him. "I'm going to be hurt by this, and there is nothing I can do about it, is there?"

"I'm so sorry. I never meant for this to happen." She nodded and rolled her hips over him again. "You will not remember me after our time together."

Kala wanted to tell him she'd remember him forever, but wasn't sure. She had an idea that Riss was different than her; she was not really sure what kind of different, but he wasn't like her. When she rolled her hips again, he ran his feather over her nipples, and she looked down at him. Pulling him up so they sat facing each other, she rode him with strong, hard strokes while he nipped at her breasts.

"Come again for me, Kala. Tighten around me until I can no longer move, and let me fill you once again with my body." Kala wrapped her arms around him and held him to her as he rolled her to her back. His body didn't just fit with hers but seemed to be a part of it. When he started to move inside of her, taking his cock nearly to the tip before punching in again, she cried out when she came. She screamed out his name for him to come with her and felt his cum as its heat filled her. Kala knew in that moment that something more had happened than two people having sex. She'd fallen in love with the stranger.

Chapter 5

"You'll be assigned another charge until we can get your arrangements made." Riss nodded, wishing that they would simply take him now and then maybe his heart would not hurt so badly. He'd left Kala in her bed not twenty minutes ago and was speaking with Tholan about what was to happen now.

"I've had sex with her." Riss had no idea why he'd said that, but now that he had, he felt that he needed to tell him everything. "Just before you called me, as a matter of fact. She had a part of me and she had used it to masturbate."

"Your charge?" Riss nodded. "You had sex with a human? Today? What were you thinking? That is against the rules."

"I enjoyed this morning so much that I had to see if I could enjoy myself again with her." He grinned at the shocked look in Tholan's face. "I did not go back the second time to have sex with her again. I went back for my feather she had. But things did not turn out as I had thought them to."

"I should say not." Tholan got up, then sat back down twice before he spoke again. "What do you think you were doing? Having sex is for humans, not us."

"It was amazing." Tholan's mouth snapped shut, and Riss continued. "I had never thought to have sex, and now that I've had it, I wish to do it over and over again. But only with her. I should very much like to go back and have a great deal of sex with her, but I know that it is not going to happen."

"Why not?" Riss smiled sadly when Tholan flushed. "I didn't mean that the way it sounded. Of course, you will not go back and have sex with her again. What would happen if Michael or the others knew?"

Riss had thought of that. A great deal as a matter of fact. He had planned to tell Michael so that he might hurry his ending along, but now all he could think about was living his final days with Kala. And in her bed.

"I do not know what to tell him. Michael has been a good friend, but he is still the one that I report to, as you are. I'm not even sure why I told you. But I cannot...." Riss got up to pace and realized that he really needed to talk to someone. "I have told her that I will not return, and when I left her, I took what I'd left behind."

"Her memories of you." Riss nodded. It had been the most difficult thing he'd ever done, and when he'd found where she thought she loved him, he had hurt all the more for it. Love was something humans did, not protectors.

"I shall confess all to Michael when we are finished here. I will ask that he not wait for the six months that he said, but to take me now. The pain of what I've done to her is overwhelming."

"Do you love her?" The question startled him into standing and he looked at Michael, who had come in without knocking, shocked. "The girl, do you love her?"

"I don't know what you mean. Love is an emotion for humans, not for us." Michael sat down and snorted at him. "She does that as well. I have heard her on several occasions."

"She is an enigma, Miss Marrow is." Riss sat down and waited for Michael to continue. When he only stared at him, Riss felt as if he had done something that could never be forgiven. Which, in a way, he supposed he had.

"I wish to have my life ended now rather than later." Michael was shaking his head before Riss could finish. "I have committed a sin, and I know that, but to have myself aching like this is beyond suffering. I should like for my life to—"

"There's a child. I cannot allow you to die with a child of yours there on earth." Riss looked at Tholan, who looked like he felt...like someone had hit him squarely between the eyes.

"Riss can't have a child. He's not human." Michael raised a brow at Tholan, who flushed. "What I mean is, there must be a mistake. A protector cannot have a child."

"But when he laid with her, he was no longer her protector, but her lover." Michael looked at him. "Did you share with her what you were? Does she know that you were sent there to watch over her and aren't human?"

"She thinks I am simply a protector, but I did not tell her anything else. But we'll have no problems if that is what you're thinking. I have taken care of her memories of me." Michael laughed again and shook his head. "I saw many things in her mind, but nothing of me being the father of her child."

"She doesn't know it yet. And she won't hear it from you." Michael laughed again. "And if you think that this will solve anything, you taking her memories, you're sadly mistaken. Kala is a good deal stronger than you think her to be."

Riss had already figured that out. She had done what she wanted when she wanted and had never asked for anything in return. Riss got up to pace, and realized at that moment that he was in over his head for the first time in all his considerable life.

"You'll punish me, no doubt." Michael nodded but smiled. Riss didn't care for that smile. It told him that he was going to hate whatever it was. Then he supposed that was the point. "When will it begin?"

"You'll start today. And you'll continue to watch over Kala as if nothing happened." Riss stared at him. "You'll not have any contact with her, physical or otherwise. No speaking to her until you are protecting her, and you'll not in any way try to dissuade any suitors that come her way."

"Suitors? You mean men coming to ask her out?" Michael said that he did. "That isn't right. She carries my child. You cannot mean that other men will be a part of his life?"

"I do. And as you have asked to be let go from here, it shouldn't matter to you at all what happens to her or the child." Michael stood up and moved toward the door. "You'll listen to what I say to you, Riss. Stay as her protector and nothing more. If you go further, I will have to go to the next step. Trust me, you do not want me to go there."

After he left, Riss sat down and tried to think about Kala and other men. He looked up at Tholan when he cleared his throat. "You should get going. I believe she is alone right now."

"He wants me to watch over her and not be with her." Tholan nodded. "And she will have other men,

men who will be with her and my child, and I'm supposed to just let it happen?"

"Look at it this way. By the time the child is born, you'll no longer be around." Riss stared at his friend as he continued. "You should really get to work."

Riss moved through the portals and ended up in Kala's kitchen. He could see that she had been busy since he'd left her and that her kitchen, for the most part, had been packed up. Riss went through the rest of the house and saw that nearly everything had been put into bags and boxes, and she now sat on the couch watching the blank television screen. He wanted to go to her and hold her, but knew that Michael would do just what he said he would. Riss watched her until someone knocked on her door.

~~~

"You shouldn't have." Kala took the bottle of wine from Dan and sat it on the counter. "I just made chili. I'm afraid that wine will be too much for such a modest pot."

"Naw, I love wine, so if you don't want it, I'll drink it." Kala tried to think what sort of glass to give Dan, as she'd already packed up the other glasses. She had no idea why she'd bothered. There was nowhere for her to unpack them.

"I've not heard from any of the places that I've applied. Have you had any luck?" When he didn't answer her, she turned to him. He was staring at her like he was pissed about something. "Dan? What's wrong?"

"Mom kicked me out." Kala raised a brow at his tone but said nothing as he continued. "She said the only reason she let me stay as long as she did was because of the cable. Now that it's gone, she said I had to be too. She made me really mad, if you want to know the truth. We argued a lot."

"I'm sorry about that. Do you have a place to stay?" She handed him the wine opener. She hadn't packed it because she never used it and was planning to leave it behind. "I have to find a place to live, too. My apartment is being renovated, and everyone has to leave for the new owners. Your poor mother will be all alone. Is she going to be okay?"

"You don't have a home anymore either?" She shook her head suddenly, slightly afraid of him. "Well, shit, Kala. I was hoping to move in with you and have a roof over my head. You really fucked that up for me, didn't you? Now what the hell am I supposed to do now, I ask you?"

She looked at him to see if he was kidding and realized then that he wasn't. Kala started to tell him that he should have been saving his money all along when the timer sounded for the corn bread. Instead of saying what was on the tip of her tongue, she excused herself and went to the kitchen. He actually thought she would let him move in with her? The man was as looney as they came.

"Hey, Kala, where you moving to?" She looked up at him from the stove. He'd moved into the kitchen, and was so close that she looked around for something to protect herself with. "I was thinking with our unemployment and all we could afford something much better than this place anyway. We can share your money and I can take care of things."

Anger surged through her, and she felt her heart pound. She was never one to get mad, but when she did, it was never pretty. Kala had a feeling that if she didn't nip this in the bud now, he'd think he could walk all over her. And Kala had had enough of people walking over her.

"You're not moving in with me." He laughed. "I'm serious. I don't know where I'm going, but it's going to be something that I can afford. And I plan to live alone. I've no intentions of having a roommate, and I most certainly don't want someone who plans to sponge off me while I work."

"You're not going to leave me on my own, are you? You'd never be able to do that to me. And even if you did, what the hell am I supposed to do all by myself? I need you to take care of me like I always thought you should. I don't have any money saved up like you do. I lived at home, for Christ's sake. I don't—" Both of them looked at the glass that shattered on the floor. Neither of them had touched it, and as far as she could tell, the windows were closed and there was no fan on. "What the fuck was that? Ghosts? Do you have ghosts here? When we live together, you're not bringing them with you."

"I don't have ghosts, and you're not living with me." She was putting the cornbread on the plate when he moved closer to her. "What are you doing?"

"Look, this is just stupid. Let me show you what a big help I can be. You're going to have to let me stay with you until we can work something out anyway. I've already got my things in the car, and once I take Mom's car back to her we'll sit down and think this through." Dan took the plate from her. "Man, this smells really good. And I love cornbread. If you keep cooking like this, I might have to wear my jammies around here just to not have to unbutton my pants after every meal."

Kala stood there staring at him for several seconds. He, however, just simply sat down and dished himself up a bowl of chili and half the cornbread. When he asked her where his drink was, she gave him another glass and the water she had chilled before she could think to tell him to get it himself. She sat down across from him and glared. He really thought she was just going to roll over and let him do as he wanted. *Well, not today*, she thought.

"There will be no talking this over. I'm not going to support you, and there is no way you're going to move your things in here until you have someplace to live. You will not be bringing your things here either." He nodded and smiled at her, and she had a feeling that he was humoring her. "I'm dead serious. I have to find me a place to live and a job. I will not have you living here with me. Nor in the new place. I like you, but I won't let you move in."

"Yeah, you will." She got up to pace as he finished off the food she'd hoped to share with a good friend. This was out of hand. "What mix do you use for this bread? This is amazing."

"I don't use a mix. What do you plan to do tonight for a place to sleep?" He looked at her couch and nodded toward it. "Oh no you don't. You're not living here. How many times do I have to say that to you before it sinks into your thick head? I'm not your maid, and I'm certainly not your mom."

When he leaned back, she thought he was going to argue with her, but he pulled out a gun and laid it on the table. He didn't say a word as he picked up his spoon and continued eating as if he hadn't just threatened her. Kala stared at it for several seconds before it dawned on her that he would get his way or he'd kill her. This was a nightmare.

"Sit down, Kala, and eat. We'll talk about this while you finish your meal. You'll need to get out tomorrow to get a job and a place for us to stay. I don't know how much longer you have to live here, but I would think it's not long beings how you've already packed up our things." She shook her head, and he nodded to the chair. "If you don't sit down, you're going to piss me off. And I'm in no mood to fuck around with you tonight. Mother is mad enough at me. And now that you've tried to ruin my good dinner, we'll just eat quietly for the rest of this meal. I don't like arguing with anyone. It gives me a headache."

Fear made her sit down, and she thought if she had to put one bite of food in her mouth she'd puke. There was no way she was going to let him stay there. Kala had a sudden thought. "Did you kill your mother because she asked you to move out?"

"What kind of person do you take me for? I would never shoot my own momma. I'd hit her a few times when she deserved it, but I'd never kill her." He took another hunk of cornbread and shoved it in his mouth. He continued talking around his food as it spilled from his lips. "Now you, on the other hand, I just hit a little. It's only fair, I think. It's not really right of you to save all that money up and not let me have a bit of it. Especially how we feel about each other. And now I find out you're looking for a new place and you're not planning to share that with me either. After all I've done for you. And the love we've shared."

"I don't love you. I liked you until this bullshit, but I don't love you. And for that matter, what have you done for me?" He snorted, and she decided right then she was never doing that again. "You've mooched off me for years and years, but I never said anything. Having me bring you in some dinner or having me pick you up some breakfast on the way in. You even had me pick up your laundry when your mother's washer was broken. You've never even offered to pay me back for any of that. Now you think that just because you're down on your luck I should take you in? You're fucked up."

"No, I'm not. I'm not crazy." He threw the bowl across the room, and it shattered on the wall. "You call me crazy again and I won't be responsible for what I do to you. I'm not fucking crazy. They just said that to me to make me have to stay there. I'm not crazy, and you take it back right now."

Kala was afraid. Terrified really. And when she tried to think what to do, she heard a small voice in her head telling her to call the police. How the hell was she supposed to manage that? Looking around the kitchen, she saw her cell phone on the counter near where Dan had thrown his bowl. Picking up the hand towel and a few paper towels, she wrapped her phone in it and went to the wall to start cleaning it up.

"Good job, Kala. You clean it up really good, okay? I never thought about us not getting our deposit back when I did that. Make sure you get it all up. We don't want them to deduct anything from our money." Taking out the phone, she laid it on the floor as she started wiping down the mess. "I'm talking to you. I need you to answer me. Kala, you'll have to speak to me sometime. We're going to be together for a long time."

She hoped that he wouldn't be able to hear if anyone on the other end spoke when she dialed 911. As soon as she heard the man answer, she started talking to Dan, hoping that the man at the dispatcher office would understand. Her voice was so shaky that she was sure he was going to hang up on her and she'd be dead when they came to redo her apartment.

"You brought that gun here to keep me in line, didn't you? You're going to shoot me and leave me for dead. I don't want to die."

Dan told her that it was his insurance that she minded him. "I won't hurt you if you'll just do what I tell you. You know you want to help me, you're always trying to help me, and I love you for it. I can't live without you, Kala, but I won't have you treating me this way either. It's not right."

"I'm not going to let you live with me, Dan Carey. I sympathize, but you're still not living here. You'll have to leave before things get more out of hand and that gun of yours goes off." Kala closed her eyes when the man on her phone spoke. She couldn't hear what he was saying but hoped he was telling her that the police were on their way.

"You'll let me or I'll plug you full of holes until you do." Dan laughed, and she heard the man on the phone ask her if she needed help. What the hell did he think she was doing here, having a party?

"Yes." She waited for Dan or the dispatcher to speak and when neither of them did she continued. "I'm afraid of you. You wave that gun around like you're planning to shoot me. Are you?"

"Not if you simply do what I want you to. I would really hate to have to hurt you, Kala, but if you don't let me live here with you, I'm going to be homeless, and I can't let that happen." She glanced at him when the chair scraped across the floor. He was coming toward her, and he had the gun.

"I said you're not living here. I don't even like you very much right now." Dan laughed just as the dispatcher told her that help was on the way. "You should know that I'm not going to go easy. I have ways to get you out. You're not living here with me.

We just worked together, and you should go back and talk to your mom. She might let you stay until you can find yourself something."

"Nah, she's set on me not staying there anymore. She's been telling me for months that I need to find somewhere else to live, but I have stuff I need to do at home. She was never on my side like you were. And as for you getting out of our arrangement, I'm sure you do. But in the event you didn't notice, I have a gun, and I'm much bigger than you." Dan laughed again. "We'll have fun, you and I. Once the unemployment runs out, you can find a job if you don't have one already, and I'll take care of the house. But we'll need to get cable again. I won't miss my shows."

"I've called the police." His laughter had her standing up. "I have. They're on their way to come and arrest you." He looked at her phone still on the floor. She hoped that the dispatcher was still there, but she wasn't sure. When her phone went black like that, she was never sure what was going on with it.

Dan stomped over and smashed her phone with his boot before he hit her across the mouth. "Why the hell would you do that? You and I are going to be living together. This is no way to start a relationship." Kala backed up when he stood up and pointed the gun at her. "You shouldn't have done that, Kala. Now you've made me mad. I'm not so nice when I'm mad."

"Neither am I. And I told you we're nothing to each other. You're a pain in the ass, and I want you out of my house." He took a step toward her again just as someone knocked on the door. When she started for it, something exploded in her head, and she fell back. It wasn't until she saw Dan moving out of the room that she realized that he'd hit her again, and this time hard enough that she could see stars.

A few seconds later, she heard shouting and then gun fire. The police had arrived, apparently. Before she knew it, she was being helped up, and someone handed her a Baggie of ice. They said she'd been out for several minutes and should go to the hospital.

"You invited him in?" If she had to answer this question once more, she was going to have to hurt someone. It had been twenty minutes since the police had arrived, and they were treating her like she was the bad guy here. "Did you know that he was unstable?"

"No, do I strike you as the type of woman who would invite a mad man into her house? We were going to have dinner together. As friends. He and I had just lost our jobs and I had thought that we'd have a laugh over it." Kala glared at the officer. "How many times do you suppose I have to answer this same stupid question before you get your head out of your ass and go look for him?"

The officer opened his mouth and snapped it closed before looking at the man near him. Kala looked, too. He was much bigger than the first officer, and he had on a suit rather than a uniform. Enough was enough. She stood up to show them out and try to figure out what the hell she was supposed to do now.

"Miss Marrow, I'm Detective Benson Anderson. Everyone calls me Benny. I understand that you're upset, but my men are only doing their job." She started to snort but just caught herself. "Where do you suppose Mr. Carey went after leaving here? And could you tell me if he had a car or not?"

"How the hell should I know where he went? As far as a car, he said he borrowed his mother's and that he had to return it before she got madder at him. Dan said his mother kicked him out. That's why he was

here. He said she had told him that without her free
cable he couldn't live there any longer." She noticed
that he looked at another man before looking back at
her. "He killed her, didn't he?"

"Mrs. Carey was found dead in her house about an
hour before you called. The neighbors called it in. They
were suspicious when her son, Daniel Carey, was
driving around in her car. Apparently, he wasn't
allowed to use it but had on occasion borrowed it, and
she'd call us in to bring it back." Kala laid the ice pack
they'd given her on the table and stood up. "Are you
going to be sick?"

Nodding, she ran to her bathroom and almost
didn't make it. There were so many cops in her place
that she had to fight her way in. After throwing up
nothing but bile, she sat on the commode and laid her
head on the counter. The feeling of warmth settled on
her shoulders.

"He could have killed me." Crying softly, she
thought about all the things that had gone belly up in
the past few days. "What am I going to do? Dan is still
out there, and he'll find me. What if he does? Then
what? Do I just shoot him and let them take me to jail?
I'd at least have a home then."

The officer had told her what had happened when
she'd been out. Dan had opened the door and
slammed him and his partner against the wall as he'd
taken off. They had ordered him to halt, but all he did
then was turn and fire at them, and his partner had
been shot in the leg. She supposed now that was the
reason the officer had been so short with her...he'd
been worried. But she'd not shot anyone and had a
nice sized bruise on her cheek to prove she'd been just
as much a victim as he'd been. Standing up, she looked
in the mirror.

"No one will hire you now unless it's another call center." Turning her face to get a better look at her face, she felt a wave of dizziness wash over her as she tried to pep herself up. It wasn't working though. "What am I going to do now?"

Leaving the bathroom after waiting in vain for her reflection to answer her, she moved back down the hall toward the kitchen. The only person there was the detective, and he was talking on a cell phone. After he hung up, he asked her to have a seat. She sat, too tired and too overwhelmed not to.

"We're going to put you into protective custody for a few days. I just heard from my office that this place is due for destruction in a few days. Is that true?" She nodded. "I have a buddy that has a truck, and as you're already mostly packed up, we'll put your stuff in storage for you as well. We don't want you more hurt until we find Carey. And this place you're going to be staying in is nice. You'll love it and have all you need to be safe."

Kala couldn't help it; she burst into tears. For the first time in what seemed like months someone was being kind to her. And when she was handed a tissue, she nodded her thanks. Maybe she'd be safe after all. At least she hoped so.

Chapter 6

"She was hurt." Tholan nodded at Riss for the ninth time. He'd been in his office for the past hour and a half going on about how he couldn't protect her from the man that had hit her. And all because they had his hands tied. "He hit her in the face with a gun. A gun that he was going to more than likely shoot her with."

"But he didn't." Riss glared at him, and Tholan sighed. "I'm sorry she was hurt. More than you can know. But I didn't put this hold on you. You did that all on your own."

"She still shouldn't be hurt." Tholan looked up when he heard his computer ding at him. He'd put out a message to the protector of Daniel Carey. They needed answers, and this was the only way to get them now. Tholan could help the police a little if they had enough information to send them where he was. It looked as if the guy had finally answered. He read Riss what was sent to him.

"Robert says that he tried to reason with him before he left his home. He'd been working on the man since he'd killed his mother. He said that it was as if he'd been talking to a wall." Tholan looked at Riss when he realized that he'd stopped pacing. "Did you know that he'd killed his own mother?"

"Not until the officer told Kala, I didn't. He just said that he'd hit her and that she'd upset him about having to move out. Does Robert know how he'd done it?" Tholan typed in the question. The answer came back as soon as he hit enter, so Tholan figured that Robert had been telling them.

"He said that he cut her throat and she bled out. And that he'd hidden her body in the basement. He'd not even bothered cleaning up the blood everywhere either. Robert said to tell you that he's so very sorry, but he'd had the neighbors call the police and had hoped that they'd be able to apprehend him before he went any farther." There was more, but Tholan refrained from telling Riss that Carey had also killed two more people since he'd left Kala's house. Riss was upset enough. "Riss, I can't tell the police directly where Daniel is, but perhaps someone will find him before he finds Kala."

"I have to protect her." Tholan nodded, not understanding this entire situation with Riss and Michael concerning the woman. "I'm going to go to Michael and see if he'll let me stay with her until the time comes for me to leave this world."

"I already asked him." Riss stared at him, and Tholan hated to tell him. "He said that if you show yourself to her again, there will be consequences. I didn't ask him what they were, but he was not happy that I came to him on your behalf."

Riss finally sat down. The man didn't look good, and, frankly, Tholan was worried for him. He knew that Riss hadn't been sleeping well, if at all, and all his time was spent on earth with the woman. Protectors needed to have down time. That was why when their charges slept, someone else watched over them until they woke. Even when she was with another, Riss watched over her.

"She needs me." Tholan didn't bother saying anything, feeling that Riss wasn't talking to him anyway. "What of my child? What will happen to him once she finds out she's with child? I never thought of anything like this happening when I took her memories of me from her. I only thought to make her forget me. It'll be hard for her to forget a child. And where will she think it came from? Certainly not from a protector."

That was all Tholan thought about actually. The woman was going to have a child by a man she had no memories of. Not to mention the man was a protector, not a human. No matter how many ways he tried to reason it out, she was still going to be a little freaked out when the time came for her to know. He knew that he would if he were in her shoes.

"I want to go over Michael's head. There is no way that this can work for anyone." Tholan had been waiting for Riss to come up with this. But he was no closer to having an answer for him than he'd been before. "What do you think?"

"I think you should take a deep breath and think about this." Riss started pacing again. "And for the love of it all, will you please sit down? You're making me exhausted just watching you."

Riss sat, but he didn't look like he was happy about it. As he sat there, Tholan thought his friend might have aged a bit...not something his kind were able to do. But Riss had, and Tholan was worried about him. When his computer dinged again, signaling that he had another message, he nearly stood up when he saw who it was from.

"Give him comfort. I will explain all to you when I can." The boss of Michael and all of them was aware of what was going on. Not a surprise, but the fact that he'd contacted Tholan was. Answering Him that he would try, he looked at his friend again.

"Do you suppose that a child will give her comfort in her later years?" As soon as the words left his mouth, Tholan knew he'd messed up. Riss looked ready to explode. "What I mean is, do you think that when you're gone she'll have something to remember...no, that won't work either. She doesn't know you were there in the first place. What if...no, not going to work either. Who will tell her that she conceived by a protector when he was in a human form?"

"You're not helping."

No kidding, Tholan thought. He was messing this up more than he could make it right.

But Riss seemed to understand as he continued. "I'm going to miss everyone, but mostly her. And as I know she'll do a good job raising my child, I still...."

When he didn't answer, Tholan started to prompt him into completing his thought. But the noise from his computer had him pause. He was to simply let his mind flow, it said. Whatever that meant.

"I would ask that you help me with something. It's nothing that will get you into trouble, but I'd like to purchase a house. A large one with a yard. Children love yards." Tholan pulled a sheet of paper toward him and started writing things down. "And a lovely view from the kitchen. My last charge would often say that a view while washing dishes was the best. I've no idea what that meant, but she was happy."

By the time the two of them had filled two pages of things to purchase, Tholan could see a difference in

Riss, and Tholan felt better as well. He was going to contact someone that worked for them on earth and have them look for a suitable house for Kala and her unborn child. There were school districts to consider, as well as neighborhoods. Who knew there was so many things to think of when buying a home? Within an hour of Riss going back to Kala, Tholan not only had three houses for him to look at, but had set up the checking account needed to procure what they needed. Tholan was whistling for the first time in decades and felt very good about all of this.

~~~

Kala sat on the couch and looked around the place she'd been hidden away in. It was nicer than her apartment and a good deal bigger, just as Benny had told her it would be. Even the furniture was lovely, and the couch she was sitting on was as comfy as her old bed. Better maybe.

"You have enough food in the fridge for a few days. Don't open the door for anyone, and don't call anyone unless it's one of us." She nodded at Detective Anderson. "Someone will be at the front desk that works for me, and another will be down the hall at all times. When someone comes to see you, or asks to see you, you'll be instructed as to what to do then via phones, okay?"

"You really think all this is necessary?" He smiled at her and nodded. "I don't. Why would he care now that I no longer live there? He'll just find someone else to live with."

"No. Not...." He sat down across from her, and she had a feeling that he didn't want to tell her this part but was only because it was necessary. "We had a chance to go through his room at his mother's home. There were things there...pictures of you and him together, ones that I'm sure after talking to you that you never posed for. Carey had taken a few pictures of you and adjusted them to depict you and him together." She looked at him, confused. "He's taken some pictures and made this entire life of the two of you together as a couple. Carey had them hanging all over his walls, from floor to ceiling, some of them nearly poster size. There were other things there as well, things that we're sure that he stole from you. Clothing, too, which we're sure that he didn't purchase. A scarf and a sweater...are you missing those items?"

She had to think. "Yes. About a year ago my sweater came up missing that I'd hung on my chair. Maybe he just...I don't know, kept it for some reason. Perhaps he was just cold and felt badly about taking it."

"He didn't use it for its intended purpose, Miss Marrow. We found semen on it as well as the scarf. Carey has been obsessed with you for years, it seems. I would say since he started working at the cable office with you." She started shaking her head, and Benny nodded. "There's more that I won't go into, but Carey has been stalking you for a very long time. From what we can piece together, his mother knew about it as well and had said something to the neighbors about his behavior. It was their understanding that the two of them, Carey and his mother, fought about it often."

"But that's been years. I mean, surely he hasn't been taking my things since then?" Anderson nodded. "Like, what else besides the sweater and scarf? If you want me to believe this, then I want more information."

"There were several used tea cups, the paper variety. We had them tested and they were yours.

They were in bags on a shelf. Some of them dated from about ten years ago, with the tea bags still in most of them. Each of them were labeled with the date and where he'd gotten it. Then there were the notes he'd put in frames. Some of them sticky notes that simply had a smiley face on them. These too were marked and dated. He'd kept everything that ever came from you. And some things that he stole to make up stories about the two of you. He had his own little world where you're concerned." Kala tried to think where he would have gotten things like the sticky notes, and remembered something from not long ago.

"I would put one on his computer when he'd called off sick. I wanted him to know that someone was thinking about him." Benny nodded at her. "I never meant any harm in it. I was simply trying to make him feel better. You think that he would have killed me?"

"Not unless you didn't do what he wanted. I'm assuming he wanted to make the relationship between the two of you real?" She nodded at his question. "We're only piecing this together now, but it looks like he'd spent a few years in a mental hospital for killing small animals as a child. Those records are sealed, of course, but the neighbors are being very helpful. Apparently Mrs. Carey told them everything. Carey also hit her on occasion. She didn't toss him out on his ass, because she needed his help with bills at first. Then she was too frightened of him to do anything. We have also found that he had another woman, besides you, that he did the same thing too. That one didn't end well."

Kala shivered. The nice and cozy room now felt as if it were full of dark, shadowy places and that Dan was going to pop out of one of them and get to her. She looked at Benny when he said her name.

"We'll get him." She nodded, not really believing him. "I swear to you we'll get him and you'll be safe."

"Why should I feel any different now than I have my entire life about being safe?" She looked around the room when he didn't answer her. "I have no job and no place to live. My life has taken on a surreal sort of tone to it, and I'm never going to feel safe again. At least when it comes to making friends at the workplace. If there ever is a workplace again."

After they left her alone, she went into the kitchen. The cabinets were indeed full, but she wasn't hungry. There were all sorts of drinks and things in the refrigerator, but none of it appealed to her either. The fruit in the bowl on the counter didn't even spark her appetite, and she sat down at the small table and pulled the small pad of paper toward her. She began writing down all the things she needed to do after she was let go.

Job headed the list. And then a place to live. There were other things to consider in both those lists, too, so she made sub lists. Under job she put several things, one of which was benefits.

The list under apartment was a bit longer. She would need furniture. The things that she had at the other place were now, as far as she was concerned, contaminated. Dan had touched them. She knew it was stupid to think that way when she had no money to really buy things with, but the thought of sitting on anything he'd touched made her skin crawl. She added disinfectant to her list of needs.

By the time she was finished, she'd filled three pages of things she needed to do. First, she had to find a place to open an account to put her checks. She'd checked twice to make sure she had them in her bag before she was able to finish up. The money was going to be the only thing that helped her out of this, she knew. She headed toward the bedroom when she felt a small touch of something along her arm. Looking around the room, she started talking. Just repeating the way to reprogram a remote at first, then how to find a pay-per-view movie.

Kala smiled when she thought of how she might look to someone, talking to herself and even going so far as to answer. But it had kept her from quitting her job most of the times she'd been upset. And she'd worked through a great many problems as a child by being able to reason with herself. Even as a child, life hadn't been a bed of roses.

"More like a bed of thorns." Pulling her oversized tee-shirt out of her luggage someone had packed for her, she pulled it over her head after undressing. "Can you imagine my life living in an orphanage with other children who were all adopted but me? It wasn't like I was weird or anything, just not as pretty as the other children, I guess. Then there was the added thing that I had this hair."

The flaming red hair she'd had as a child had darkened as she'd gotten older. It was still red, but now it was more of a soft red rather than the carroty color she'd had long ago. Then there were the freckles. Those, too, had faded, but she still had them all over her body, and at times she wondered if she had more than her fair share.

"I always thought that I'd been put in line several times to get them when I was made. But then, I guess it was all right. It gave me something for the other children to make fun of me about other than my eyes." Looking in the mirror over the dresser, she looked at them now. "How do you suppose this particular shade of purple was invented for a person? It's almost like I have black eyes rather than simply purple. Not to mention there is no choice for them on any form. Blue, green, and brown are the standards. Sometimes I'd see other, but you couldn't put the color purple in there. I wonder why."

Not that she cared all these years later. She just waited for people to get over looking at them before she'd continue with what she wanted to say. Smiling, she thought of the reaction of the first boy she'd kissed.

"He'd claimed that my eyes darkened. Whoever heard of such a thing? Darkening indeed. He was more than likely trying for a compliment to get into my pants. Fat lot of good it did him. All he managed to do was tick me off." She moved back to the living room and sat down again, picking up the remote. "I wonder what on earth Dan is doing right now?"

He'd tried to kill her. Or he would have had she not called the police. And why she'd done that was beyond her as well. Never in all her life had she done something like that, calling the police in a situation where she should have.

"I'd been scared and only heard that voice of reason because of that." She no more believed that than she did the police would keep her safe. "Things always happen to me. I'm always the one that will get hurt if there is a way or lose if there is any change. I have that knack about me."

Finally, after an hour of not really watching the television, she went to bed, and almost as soon as her eyes closed, she saw Dan's face again. The rage in it and the way he'd stormed after her when he'd hit her. But as soon as she decided that she needed to get up, a soft wave of security seemed to wash over her, and she felt herself drifting off to sleep. The man from before, the dream of the feathered man, came to her almost immediately.

"Are you in a better frame of mind to believe in me, my child?" She didn't answer Him but looked around the entirely white room. "I love the peacefulness of this kind of space. There is so much going on now that…well, I need a place to come where it's quiet."

"You're not real." He only shrugged at her. "Do you have a name, or do you want me to refer to you as Feathered Jerk?"

He laughed at her, and she felt stupid. But before she could tell Him she was sorry, He put up His hand and stopped her. She didn't have any idea why, but she liked Him better this time.

"I'm glad you do. And most of the people who know me call me Boss. You may do so if you'd like." She nodded, not sure, but she thought the man enjoyed the name for what it was rather than a title. "Do you know that I enjoy coming here to talk to you?"

"I'm nothing all that special." He laughed again and told her she was mistaken. "I'm just a woman. Unless you're referring to my long line of crappy luck."

"No, I was thinking about how refreshing you are to speak to. Most people want to not look at me, and they tend to stumble all over their words rather than simply treat me as someone that cares about them." He leaned forward in His chair, and she smelled honey and lavender. "It's the scent that grows along my place. You'd like it there, I think. But not for some time yet. You have work to do."

"Riss." He smiled and nodded at her. "You told me that I would meet a man, and I saw his name on a file."

Again He nodded and smiled at her. "You have met him. But he is…how shall I say…he's not ready for you as yet. You are him, but that is a different matter altogether."

"I don't understand. And…I can remember the name, but you say I've met him?" Boss nodded and leaned back. Kala had a feeling He wanted her to work it out, but her mind was somehow blocked.

"I could help you with that, but then he will know that you and I have conversed about him. And that cannot be just yet. But I will tell you that your trials are not yet over. You'll have much more to go through before he can come to you again. But I have a feeling that you'll do fine." Kala started to snort and stopped herself.

"I've been through a great deal already. Did you know that a man tried to kill me? Well, not really kill me, but he did come to my house and hit me." She watched Him lean forward again, and He touched her face. The pain she'd felt earlier was now gone. Touching her face, she felt the warmth. "You healed me."

"Not really. What I have done was take away the pain for now. I'm sorry, but again we cannot allow Riss to know that I've been here. He will be most unhappy with me."

The file appeared in front of her again. This time it was open for her, and there were words there. Picking it up, she looked at what it said, then looked at Boss.

"It says here that I'm to have a child. I haven't had sex in a very long time, and I'm pretty sure that's not going to happen." He leaned back and gestured toward the file. This time she saw a picture and ran her fingers down the cheek of the man there. "Is this Riss?"

"It is. He is also the father of your child. You are carrying it now." Kala put her hand over her flat belly and shook her head as he continued. "I'm sorry, but it is true. Riss knows of him, but I am keeping him from you for just a little while longer. I need him to...disobey me once more concerning you. You'll have to trust me when I tell you it will be worth your while."

She looked at the man in the photo before putting the file back down. "I don't want a child right now. Maybe never. I don't have time for one, and I certainly don't have the money to raise one on my own."

"You'll be fine. And I'm sorry to tell you, my child, but you already carry the babe within your womb. Riss and you have been...together...several times. And as a human, he was able to give you this child."

"Human?" Boss nodded. "I don't understand. He's not human? If not, then what the hell is he?"

"A protector. Yours, as a matter of fact. He was sent here to protect you and to guide you, but I have changed it for the two of you. Riss wishes to be let out of my services, and I will need to find him somewhere to go after I do. Do you understand?" She shook her head. "You are a clever young woman. I'm sure that it will occur to you once you have had a chance to meet him again."

"I don't know what's going on." He didn't say anything, and Kala got up to pace as she worked through what was going on. "I'm betting that when I wake, I'll not remember any of this, will I?"

"You will remember what you wish to remember." She wanted to hit Him over the head with something. But all that was in the large room was two chairs and a table that they both had been sitting at. "You are not happy with me, are you?"

"No, I'm not. You're talking in circles and expect me to get it later. Well, I don't have until later. There's a mad man out to kill me." Boss nodded at her, and Kala decided that whatever it was she'd had to eat today, she was—something occurred to her. "There was a feather. I had one in my hand, and I was using it...."

Flushing, she felt her face heat up when He laughed. "You did indeed. Most people would have simply tossed it away, but you found its one use that no one else has. It was the bond between the two of you that brought you to the point where you are now. I would hope that you'd be able to summon Riss when this is finished, but I believe your connection now is as solid as anyone's."

"I want to wake up." He stood up, and she took a step back when His wings spread wide behind Him. "Riss has wings as well?"

"He does. And someday I will allow him to tell you all about them. It's time for you to wake now, Kala. There is a man awaiting you in your living room, and I'd wish very much for you to trust him as well. His name is Michael."

Then He was gone, and Kala woke with a start. The room was dark as the night, and she felt suddenly terrified at what might be in the room with her. The dream was fading, but she knew that a man was coming to talk to her. How she knew, she had no idea, but he was coming. Getting up, she pulled on her robe to go into the living room. He was standing there with a box in one hand and a large folder in the other.

"You must be Michael." He nodded and smiled. "Do you have wings as well?"

And when they seemed to sprout behind him, she grabbed the back of the couch. "I'm not in Kansas anymore, am I?"

His laughter was not reassuring.

Chapter 7

Dan moved through the room slowly. He had a feeling that someone was watching him, but couldn't find anyone other than the man he'd tied to the chair. Dan was pissed off, and things never looked right when he was this mad. And he wanted to find his Kala and have her help him through this. Whenever she was around him, he felt calmer and his head didn't pound so hard. Everything just seemed better when she was around.

They'd taken her from him. The police had come to their home and had taken her away for some reason. And now he couldn't find her. He looked over at the man he thought was responsible and laughed when he cringed. Maybe he'd make him tell him what was going on with her.

"You should never have fired us. I tried to tell you when you was coming out of your office, but you wouldn't listen. I really needed you to listen to me." Randy Shields moaned when Dan popped him in the head again using his fist. Randy had been the one who had signed his and Kala's emails. It was all his fault that Dan was now running around trying to find his one true love.

The gag in Randy's mouth prevented Dan from understanding him, but Dan got it. He was begging again. Dan hated when people begged. His mother begged him all the time. Take out the trash, answer the phone...stuff that she should have been doing for him. Not the other way around. He'd been the one working, while she sat around in her wheelchair ordering him around like he wasn't anybody important.

"I'm going to have to have you go into your office tomorrow and call her for me so I can tell her it's okay to come home. Kala needs to come back to work for you guys, but the place where she is staying is being watched by the cops so I can't tell her it's okay. Everything is okay now. That way I can get our new address. She probably forgot to leave it for me." Dan sat down at the table and looked around the room. "This is a nice house you got here. You think maybe Kala would like it? I don't know what she can afford to pay, but I'm really thinking this would be something she should look into. There is a lot of room for all my cable stuff and my notes and stuff."

Randy started talking again, but Dan ignored him. He never said anything worth listening to anyway, even if he could understand him. And when Dan saw the blood on the floor, he got up to look at where it might be coming from. The other room was a mess compared to the dining room he and Randy had been talking in. Dan went into the room with his gun out just in case someone was hunting him again. Those damned police.

The den, he supposed it was called, had broken furniture all over the place, and there was more than just the blood on the floor. There were splashes of it over the walls and across the pictures that hung on them. He looked around, wondering if he'd hurt himself, and started patting down his body for wounds. Then he saw her, or at least her legs hanging out from under the broken table.

The woman looked as if someone had beaten in her face, Dan noticed when he got closer to her. And when he took a step closer still to her, he could see that not only had it been her face but her entire head as well. Most of the back of it had been beaten in, and there was what looked like brain matter on the floor by her. He looked at the rest of her body, but stepping around the table she was under, he could see that her arms and legs looked badly beaten as well. Someone had hated this woman. Going toward the opposite door, he found what appeared to be a dog, too. This one someone had cut up and removed his head from his big body. Dan was sickened by the sight, and had to leave the room now or throw up everywhere.

Going back into the kitchen, he stood near the sink with the cold water running over his wrists to try and make himself feel better. The sight in the other room had been too much. Then he noticed the blood on the rags that were laying on the sink and in it.

"Somebody hurt that woman," Dan said. The man whimpered loudly, and Dan went to stand in front of him. "Did you know her? The woman in the other room, did you know who she was? I gotta tell you, she's been beaten worse than I ever saw anyone before."

When the man started talking, Dan reached over and pulled the tape off his mouth. The tears running down his face made Dan want to hit him. Men did not cry. He'd heard that most of his life. Randy started talking so fast that Dan had to ask him to slow down.

"You murdered my wife. You did it." Dan started to shake his head, but Randy nodded as he continued. "You took the ball bat to her head the moment she came into the room, and when I tried to help her, you hit me until I lost consciousness. You murdered my wife."

"No. You've got it all wrong. I'm not allowed to kill anyone. They said if I did, then I'd have to go back." Dan started pacing around the table as Randy sobbed. "I've never killed a person before. They told me that when I hurt that kid that I could have, but I've never hurt anyone since. Not even when they put me in that terrible place."

Dan felt his body turn cold at the thought of the place he'd been taken as a teenager. The little boy hadn't died, so he could never understand why he'd been chained to the bed and left there to die. Of course, after several months he'd been freed. His momma had come and got him and took him to the house, but she'd told him if he hurt again, he was never coming back to stay with her. He'd even promised her on the Bible.

"Do you know what they did to me? They put electricity to my ears and balls. They told me that I was a degenerate. I'm not that." He'd had to look the word up when his momma had told him what it meant. He'd never believed her, but it turned out while she wasn't really giving him the real definition, she'd told him that he was a monster.

When Randy continued to cry and whine about him killing his wife, Dan started explaining to him how he knew he'd not done those horrible things. "I'm not depraved, immoral, and corrupt, or perverted either. I got standards, and I take my medications."

He hadn't taken them for a long time, but he'd been well for so long that he felt that taking them was stupid. Dan had even started to stockpile them in the event that he might need them later again. But when he'd accumulated over a thousand of the pills he'd had to take four times a day, he'd stopped and dumped them in the toilet. He often wondered if there was a big alligator somewhere all doped up.

Dan sat down at the table and looked at Randy as he kept crying like he'd hurt him, and going on and on about his dead wife. It was making Dan's head hurt again, and when that happened, he would go black. He hated not remembering what happened to him when he'd go black.

"Shut up." As soon as Randy's mouth snapped closed, Dan got up to pace again. There was something too wrong about all of this, he was going to get to the bottom of it. Now, right now.

"The police were here, huh? That's who did this? You called them when you saw me at the door? They'd do something like this to blame it on me." Randy was shaking his head, then was accusing Dan again of killing his precious wife. "You know you can tell me the truth. I won't be mad at you. Just tell me who came in here and beat that woman up."

"You did it, you motherfucking asshole. You came into my house with a bat and hit her when she opened the door. My poor Connie never did anything to anyone, and now you've killed her. I'm going to make you pay for this." Dan started to hit Randy again when he realized that was what he wanted. He wanted something else to blame on him.

"Well, I'm not going to do it. You can just fuck off. We both know what happened, and I had nothing to do with that shit in the other room. The dog either." Randy tried to pull at the tape on his wrists that Dan had put around them to keep him in the chair. "You can't get up just yet. I need you to call Kala."

"I don't know how to get in touch with her. I've told you this several times. I wrote the letter a long time ago. It's a form letter that they send out when they have to let someone go. I had nothing to do with you or this Kala person receiving it. I don't even know anyone by that name." Dan snorted and hit him again. "I swear to you, I don't know."

He was getting on his nerves, and Dan had to go to the door and open it again. He'd been doing that for his entire life when he was really overwhelmed like he was now. It helped him to work something out by breathing in the fresh air. Dan supposed it had something to do with being locked up in the bad place, but he couldn't think while he was feeling this way. When the urge to hurt seemed to lessen, he turned to look at Randy again. But someone had gotten to him while Dan had been breathing in the cool air.

Randy's head was laying in his lap, blood streamed from his open neck like a geyser, and Dan felt his belly jump. And he would swear that Randy was looking at him with those blank, dead eyes. Picking up the placemat from the table, Dan tossed it over the face and watched in horror as blood soaked through it in seconds. Dan moved out of the house and into the yard, where he threw up several times before he finally fell into the bush he'd used.

"Someone is trying to make it so I have to go back. I won't do it. Never ever never ever again." Dan sat up and looked around, reasoning that whoever did this to Randy would be close enough to do the same to him. Moving deeper into the hedge line of bushes, he waited for several minutes to see if anyone had seen him.

Dan knew that he'd have to do something and soon. Whoever was stalking him was going to get him into deep trouble, and then Kala would be all alone. He didn't want that for her. When she'd told him stories about her life as a kid, he knew that he wanted to keep her well-loved and happy. She'd not had a good life, but Dan was going to give her one. They'd be happy for the rest of their lives.

Going back into the house, he tried his best to ignore the blood that had pooled under the chair where Randy was sitting. Whoever had done this had left their knife behind, and Dan eyed it. It had to be the biggest knife he'd ever seen. It looked like one of those swords that people hung on their walls in the movies he watched. And as much as he wanted to touch it, he knew that he'd leave fingerprints. That wasn't going to help him if he ever had to go to the police about this…which he just decided wasn't going to happen. Going back to the sink, he noticed that his hands were covered in blood again, and so was his shirt. He needed to clean up or he'd be pulled over quickly if anyone saw him.

Dan thought about going back to his momma's house, but something kept him from thinking along those lines. He knew that she'd kicked him out, but she'd done that before and he'd been able to talk her into letting him come back. But he had a feeling this time wasn't going to be that easy. He'd done something there that would have her pissed off at him for a few more days. And when she was that mad at him, he knew that his chances of changing her mind were going to be slim. No, his best bet was to go to Kala's house and get him something to wear from his drawers.

As he went up to take a shower, making sure he didn't touch anything to leave fingerprints, Dan tried to think where his Kala might be. Her apartment building had more police than he'd ever seen in it, and he wasn't comfortable going in there. He'd tried all their favorite restaurants, and also the movies. But no one there had seen her. He wanted to go back to his house and get his pictures of them there together, but again it meant going to his momma's house, and he wasn't going there yet.

When he found the bathroom, he also found some shirts and a pair of pants lying on a bed and picked them up gingerly. Dan was surprised to find they might fit him. Stripping down to his skin, he stepped into the shower stall before turning on the water. He loved the feeling as the water went from icy cold to so hot it scorched his skin. Reaching for the bottle of shampoo on the ledge, Dan was concerned when bloody water streamed down the drain, but knew that somehow it had nothing to do with the body, nor any wounds on him. He washed himself three times before he finally just stood under the spray to rinse.

"Someone is trying to frame me." The echo of his voice in the silent room had him grinning. "I've watched enough television in my life to know that I'm not being paranoid but stating facts. Someone is really trying to frame me, and it's all to keep me from my Kala."

After getting out of the shower and drying himself, he dressed in the underwear and socks he'd pulled from Randy's drawer. When he was reaching for a clean shirt, he found the remote. Picking it up, he was surprised to find one of his shows on and sat on the edge of the bed to watch it. Then before he knew it, there were three more of his programs on, and he settled on the bed fully to relax. It was nearly one in the morning when he finally left the Shield house.

He didn't even feel bad that he'd taken the families money that had been on the dresser, and the keys to the car in the garage. His thinking was that neither of them were going to need them, and he'd only borrow them until he found his Kala. As soon as he looked in the back seat, he had to smile. Taking some extra clothes and some snacks was the only reasonable thing to do, as well as the cell phone and a few bottles of good wine. It hadn't been very nice of them to make him look for them, he thought with a frown. When you invited someone to your house to stay, the very least you should do was show them around to where the good stuff was hidden. But he had enough for him and Kala to enjoy. She'd love it, Dan just knew it.

~~~

Riss waited for Robert to come into the office with him and Tholan, but he was running behind, Tholan had told him. Riss didn't care, he just wanted to get back to the house and watch over Kala. She hadn't been sleeping well, and he wanted to comfort her while she did so. When the door opened just as Riss was going to ask again if he could leave, he knew something had gone terribly wrong. As soon as Robert walked in the door, Riss had to sit down. It was that or fall over.

"He's killed two more people." Riss looked at Tholan when Robert didn't continue right away. Tholan didn't look any better at the news than Riss felt. The man, Daniel Carey, needed to be stopped.

"What have you done to get him help?" Help? Riss looked at Tholan when he asked. The man didn't need help, he needed to be brought over so he could be dealt with.

"I've done all I can, but he is thinking on a plane that is no longer one I can reach. Today when he took a knife to a man's head and removed it from his shoulders, I felt my connection to him sever as well. He is all alone now, and I've no way to reach him."

Riss had heard of this before, but in his experience by the time they got this far from them, the protector had already made arrangements to get help. Before he could ask Robert who he had brought, Tholan answered his unspoken question.

"We're so shorthanded now. I'm so sorry that I couldn't get you someone sooner, Robert, but I did try. I'm guessing that Arryn couldn't do much either?" Robert shook his head. "I'm not sure what else we can do. I've done all I can from here. I'm sorry. I truly am. Perhaps our best bet now is to make sure that he doesn't get to the girl. At all costs, we must keep her safe. Do you suppose he knows where Miss Marrow is?"

"No, he doesn't know. But he is obsessed with her to the point of thinking that all the things that he's imagined between them are real now. Before, he would have days where he could reason with himself that they were not a couple, but he's beyond that now. He's even gone as far as to tell the restaurant that he'd been to with his mother that it was Kala that had been with him. He'd been there to see if they'd seen her, and all they could recall was him and an older woman. Mr. Carey got very upset with them until they called the cops. But he was long gone by the time they arrived." Robert looked at him. "Riss, I'm so sorry about this. I've tried my best to get him to understand, but he was gone long before this. If I could have gotten through to him today I would have, but he is stronger than me now. His mind is no longer open to suggestions that I can use to get him to see reason."

Riss wanted to go to Kala even more now. But he knew that without enough information as to where this man had gone, he wouldn't know how to protect her. Instead of asking Robert why he didn't ask for help sooner, he nodded his understanding and asked him if he remembered anything else. He thought about what Robert had already told him, and he was more afraid for Kala now than ever before.

"I've asked Sheppard to have the neighbors call the police. He's the protector watching over their new baby, and was nearby when I came away from the house. When I left, he was having their neighbor go over with the thought of borrowing a cup of milk. It was all we could think of. The front door is unlocked and standing slightly open, so hopefully she'll see enough to call the authorities but not go inside. It's a mess."

A mess. Riss tried not to think about the mess that had been made in killing two people. He did think about the one and only time he'd been assigned a serial killer. Even as a child, he had been hard to control, but as he grew older and stronger, there was little that Riss could do on his own. He'd left bodies of women everywhere he'd gone, killing them in such a brutal way that it was hard for the humans to figure out who they might have been. Finally, he and Tholan had decided to bring in Michael. It didn't end well for any of them. The man had finally killed himself and became beyond their realm then. He was sure this wasn't going to end well for a great many people, either.

"Do you suppose we should bring in Michael? He would be able to connect with him more than we could." Tholan was shaking his head even before Riss finished speaking.

"We've tried that already. Michael went to him just yesterday. All the man kept doing was rocking back and forth and saying a nursery rhyme over and over...the one where the cow jumped over the moon."

Tholan got up to pace, and Riss watched him as he continued speaking. "We've tried all we can think of. That's why I've brought you here, Riss. I need for you to take someone with you from now on to watch over Kala. It's important that she live."

Riss knew that to be true. She was carrying his child, but he thought maybe Tholan meant something else. But he thought of something before he could ask about what he'd meant...the house.

"She will have a better chance at the house I'm purchasing for her." Robert looked at him oddly, but Riss didn't care. This was his woman and his babe. "There I will be able to watch over her without anyone knowing that she lives there. The police are doing a fine job so far, but I believe she will need more than they can offer before this is finished. At least this home is protected in a way that the police cannot."

"But you've not closed on anything, have you?" Riss shook his head. The people selling the home he wanted were being too slow. He was nearly ready to move on to another house if they didn't respond about his offer. But this one he loved for his child and Kala. "Then we'll have her stay where she is for now. They may not have your power, Riss, but they will do better than you can alone if she is not in an enhanced home."

Riss had been given permission to have the home he was purchasing for Kala secured, meaning that some of his power was surrounding the house and property at all times....including after he was gone. Riss tried not to think about his own death now. It hurt him in ways he'd never dreamed it would. And it was no longer the thought of leaving behind his child. To leave Kala was more painful than the thought of his friends he'd had since the beginning.

"Riss?" He looked at Tholan and realized he must have been talking to him for some time. He also noticed that Robert was gone. "You okay?"

"Yes. No." Riss took a deep breath and let it out slowly before answering again. "I honestly don't know. I feel good when I'm with her and empty when I'm not. Am I supposed to feel this way in this new program that we're in? If so, then I don't think it will work. It's much too painful."

Riss hoped so, but he had a feeling it was all him. He wanted to hold her, to touch her again. Keep her in his arms for all times. The child would be his, and he found that he wanted to watch it grow within her belly, touch him when he moved. He wanted to play with the babe, take him on long walks with his mother, and do things that he'd seen humans do with their own children.

"It's not. I'm sorry, Riss, but what you're experiencing is just something you have done on your own. I'm not sure that it's love, but it is something very close." Tholan sat down as he continued. "How is she doing with all this? I know that you can't speak with her, but you must hear what she says to the others around her."

"She is…she is Kala. I've never met a stronger woman. All this going on around her and she seems to be doing well. There are times when I can feel her sadness, but before I can speak to her about it, she brings herself around and is better for it." Riss smiled. "I think she is doing better than I am, if you want to know the truth."

"And have you stayed out of her reach?" Riss nodded. "Good. I am still trying to think of ways for you to be with her before you die, but I'm not having any luck with it. Michael said that things are in motion, and changing them now would have too much of a ripple effect on other things."

The same thing he'd told him the other morning. Riss had made a mistake with this quitting thing, several as a matter of fact, and now he was going to have to live with them. He wished so many times that he'd not met Kala, but he also thought of how much richer the last days of his life would be because of her being in it. When Tholan's phone rang, Riss left him. It was about time for him to go back to earth anyway.

Chapter 8

Kala sat at the table. She had gotten up from the bed for some reason, and now all she could think about was feathers. Stupid thing was that all the pillows in the apartment she was staying in had foam in them, not a single feather to be found anywhere. She had even tried the comforter and found that it was made with some sort of thick padding. Things were going from weird to weirder all the time. Then there was the box that she'd found that morning. She had a vague idea that she'd talked to someone about it, but for the life of her couldn't think who it had been.

Within it were all sorts of things she knew didn't belong to her. There was a man's shirt, as well as a medallion on a gold chain. But it was the medallion that she continued to think about. It was gold with small jewels surrounding it. Most of them she knew, but there were several that she did not. And in the center of it was a man dressed in what appeared to be something from ages ago, an outfit that she knew was something he would have worn to war, complete with a breastplate and helmet. He held a shield in one hand and a sword in the other, and around his head, it appeared that he had a halo, one made of gold.

She had put the long chain around her neck and hadn't been able to take it off since she'd put it there. For some reason it made her feel warm and safe. The shirt now lay on her bed, and she'd not even bothered to wonder why she'd had the urge to sleep in it. She knew that as soon as she retired for the night it was going to be the only thing she had on. And if those two things weren't strange enough, there was the file.

In it were houses for sale...not just pictures, but specs for each of them. One of them, the one she had loved the moment she'd seen it, was a nice, big farmhouse with a hundred acres around it, with five bedrooms, four baths, and a kitchen she could see herself baking all sorts of things in. The entire house had been updated too; big closets in every bedroom, the bathrooms with all new showers, and the master bath had a large claw-foot tub, just like the ones she'd seen as a kid. And the yard. She could see a swing set in the front, a large sand box in the rear, dogs and cats running through the barn, and fields with the children.

Sighing heavily, she closed the folder on the pipe dreams and put it under the place mat. Kala knew that things like this were never going to be in her cards, and she might as well give up on it now. Getting up, she went to the fridge to get a glass of water and turned to see a man standing in the kitchen with her. As freaky as it was, she wasn't afraid of him or the fact that she had no idea how he'd gotten into the apartment with her.

"Hello. Do I know you?" She'd been introduced to all the cops before they started watching her. Just last night she'd met the newest man, and he'd not been overly fond of her, she could tell. There was something so...she wanted to say evil, but that wasn't right either. As much as she'd hated to do it, she'd asked Benny to have him removed from her detail.

"No, you shouldn't. My name is not important. What is important is why I'm here. Did you pick out a house yet?" She glanced at the folder and then back at him. "I need to get things started for the other end. Could you tell me which it was?"

"Other end?" She looked again at the folder, then back at him. "I'm sorry. What does me liking a house have to do with anything? It's not another safe house, is it? I like this one very much, and I'm afraid if you took me to any of those houses there, I'd never want to leave."

"It won't be necessary for you to. Things are progressing quickly now that I have narrowed it down." She was slightly confused by his statement, but when he reached for the folder, she waited for him to say something else as he looked over the different pictures. "This one?"

She nodded, and he smiled. "I don't know why they'd let me pick out my own house. It's not as if I could afford it or anything."

The folder seemed to disappear, but she didn't comment. Actually, she was sort of afraid to. Not that this man looked like he was going to harm her...just the opposite as a matter of fact. She found she wanted to be with him in an "I need you to keep me safe" sort of way. When he smiled at her, she flushed.

"What the fuck is going on?" He laughed but didn't answer her. "I mean, I have all these weird feelings over the past few days, like I need to be held. I'm not a person who generally feels the need for people to hug me. And then there's the houses and me picking them out. The shirt on my bed is another thing I don't understand. Whose is it? And where did it come from? And feathers. I need a feather."

"Feather?" the man asked. Kala nodded. "I see. And this need for the feather, do you have any idea what you would do with it once you had one?"

She felt her face heat up, but he didn't seem to notice, or if he did, he didn't seem to be going to comment. Sitting down at the table, she waited for him to either pop out of her life or sit with her. Either way, she was having a nervous breakdown soon.

"I have the strangest dreams, too. Of a man making love to me." She looked up at him when she realized what she'd said. "I'm sorry."

"No worries. You need someone to talk to, and your protector is unable to do it with you." He seemed to look over her shoulder, and she turned, too. When she looked back at the man, he was smiling at her. "I think he loves you very much."

"Who?" She felt her body heat up...not sexually, but with a warmth all the same. When she looked back, there was no one there, of course, and turning back, the man was gone as well. And so was the paperwork on the house.

Kala sat there for a long time. She heard the doors open and close down the hall, and then one of the men came in to use the bathroom. But still, she sat. Benny came in a while later, and she grinned at him. The man had a way about him that had her wanting to tease him into a smile.

"You've been absent from my daily watchers." He nodded at her and smiled back as she continued. "I've been thinking that this whole thing isn't necessary. I think that as soon as it could be arranged, I'd like to—"

"There's been another two murders."

Kala felt her skin tighten on her body. She was wishing now that she'd not told Benny to stop treating her with kid gloves and to tell her straight up what the hell was going on. She didn't want him beating around the bush anymore. "A couple was killed in their home not a block from here. We're not sure if it's just a coincidence or planned, but we're tightening our circle around you."

"He killed a couple? Are you're sure it was him?" Benny nodded. "I can't believe he's doing this. Dan always seemed so...well, I guess normal. But that's not quite right either. I think in the back of my mind I sort of knew he was a little stranger than normal. But I guess I didn't want to believe it of him. And now he's chasing me, and no one seems to have a fucking clue as to why. Do you know? Do you know why me?"

"I'm sorry, Kala, I don't know. And if asked, he more than likely doesn't know either. It could be that you were in the right place at the right time in his life. Or it may be that you reminded him of someone long ago. It's hard to tell." He laid the newspaper on the table between them, but she didn't reach for it as she had every time he brought her one. "If it makes you feel any better, I've taken the front section out and only left you the ads."

Taking the paper, she nodded her thanks as he got up to leave. She was looking for the help wanted section when she heard him say her name. Looking up, she could see that he was as exhausted as she'd ever seen anyone look.

"Don't open the door for anyone. And my men will no longer be coming in here to use the bathroom or for any other reason except for when you call them. I don't want to leave you in a position where you simply don't know." Kala thought about asking him if ghosts counted, but didn't. He would have her locked up if she did. He continued as if she were as sane as he was. "Kala, we'll have to work together on this. All of us. Once he's caught, and he will be, we'll need to keep you out of the papers or others will come for you too."

"Come for me? What do you mean 'others will come for me'? Why?" She thought she knew the answer to her own question, but he answered her before she could say it.

"Because there are a lot of sick people out there and they'd love to have their name attached to his, no matter what the circumstances are surrounding it. Fame is fame to some of these nut balls." Kala nodded. "Lock the door with the chain. And when you retire tonight, make sure that you put a chair under the knob. It won't keep him out if he's determined to come in, but it will slow him enough that my men can get here. There is no reason for you to take chances."

After Benny left, she decided to take a long, hot bath. Whatever jobs might be out there for her were not going to wait on Dan getting caught. She didn't want to think of what was in store for him now. After killing so many people, he would be lucky if he ever made it to jail, much less a trial. She hoped that someone caught up with him before he got to her., because now she knew that it was no longer an issue of if he would get to her, but when. As she slipped into the hot water, she started talking to herself.

"Can you imagine me having that house? All those lovely trees and so much yard?" Giggling, she thought if anyone could hear her now, they'd think she was just as looney as Dan. Minus the murdering, of course. "And that kitchen. I know I keep coming back to it, but I have always wanted a big kitchen. With a window over the sink. The lady at the orphanage used to tell me when I would sneak in there that having a window over the sink is like having a window to the world. I guess she could see things I couldn't out hers, but that's okay. It made her happy."

Shaving her legs, she felt the water slide over her skin, and her body heated with need. The man in her dreams would know what to do, and she wanted to close her eyes and wait for him. But there was no way she was going to sleep now. She'd be awake way before the sun if she did.

"Kala girl, you're not used to all this idle shit. You need a job." Laughing, she thought about something crafty to do, and for the life of her couldn't think of a single thing. There had been this girl at the cable company that could take other people's pictures and put them in an album that seemed to come alive with stickers and stuff. She could barely remember to print hers when she wanted a copy of them, and had simply kept them on her old cell phone. Which reminded her, she had to see about paying her bills soon. Even though she no longer had one thanks to Dan, she still had bills to pay.

"I wonder how I can do that. Pay my bills, I mean. Do you think they have a courier service that will take my money to get money orders so I don't get…wait, I don't have an electric bill anymore." Giggling again, she lay back in the water and closed her eyes. "I guess all I have is the cell bill and my car insurance for a car that will have to be junked if I have to do any more repairs on it."

After about another hour of just relaxing, Kala got out. She'd been putting in more hot water every fifteen minutes or so, and now she was all pruney. Getting out, she dried off and pulled the shirt that she'd found over her head. As soon as she did, a man appeared with her.

~~~

It took him a few seconds to realize that she could see him. Riss took a step back when she put out her

105

hand to touch him and bumped into the dresser behind him. Kala put her hand on his arm, and he felt it all the way to his toes.

"Riss?" He nodded, not sure what to do now. He'd not revealed himself to her, but somehow she could still see him. "Is this your shirt?"

"I think it might be." He touched the button on the front and felt her warmth seep into his fingers. "How did you get it?"

"I don't know. It just showed up." Kala took another step to him, and her body was nearly flush with his. Before he could think he was going to pay for touching her, he cupped his hand on her bottom and pulled her closer still.

"I shouldn't be doing this." She nodded as she nuzzled her nose into his throat. "Kala, love, you need to take a step back from me."

"No. I want you. I don't know why I do, but I want you more than I've ever wanted anyone before." She rocked into his hard cock and moaned before continuing. "Please, Riss. Take me."

His mouth touched to hers, and he felt her tongue run along his lips. Opening for her, he turned her when her mouth seemed to devour his. Now that her back was against something firmer, he picked her up and felt her legs wrap around him. Riss lifted his head to look down at her.

"I can't leave you." She nodded and reached for the buttons on his shirt. As soon as she had the first two opened, she kissed his flesh, heating it to the point where it was almost painful. The more skin she exposed, the more she tasted of him.

The buttons on his shirt she had on didn't stand a chance against his need of this woman. They pinged all over the room and dresser until there was none left on the shirt. Opening it slowly, he watched as it caught on her hard nipple and made him whimper.

"Suck on my nipple, Riss. I need to feel your mouth on me." He did as she'd begged him and lifted her higher so he could pull the shirt off. When she was naked, he turned and started for the bed. As soon as her back touched the spread, he stood up to tear his own clothes off.

"Let me." She helped him undo his belt and pulled it free of the loops almost in the same motion. When she started for his snap and zipper, Riss reached for the post at the end of the bed and held on while she kissed and licked her way to his boxers. When she freed his cock, her mouth took him deep, and it was all Riss could do not to cry out his pleasure.

"Kala, love." Curling his fingers into her hair, he meant to pull her back, but she swallowed around him then and he held her to him. It was that or fall over. She was doing things to him that made his eyes cross. And when she cupped his now naked balls and squeezed them, Riss cried out her name and begged her to stop.

"I need to be inside of you." She took him again, this time watching him as she bobbed up and down on his shaft. The faster she went, the harder he began to rock into her. Riss felt his balls tighten up and knew that he was going to release soon, but she pulled back and laid out on the bed.

"I want to feel you inside of me too." She opened her legs and he could see how wet she was. "We've done this before, haven't we? We've had the most amazing sex and then you left me."

"Yes, we have, love. And I had no choice." She nodded and slid her hand down over her pretty mound and then slid her fingers into her heat. "You're going to make me release all over you if you keep that up."

"Please do. I want to feel your hot cum on my body. Then I want you to fuck me hard." Nodding, he fisted his cock as she continued to slide in and out. When she cupped her breast in her free hand, Riss decided that he wanted to drink from her again. Crawling up the bed on his knees, he pulled her legs open as wide as he could get them and leaned into her. She smelled of heat and sex.

The first swipe of his tongue made him moan. But when her legs tightened around his head, he looked up at her from his position and nearly came from the sight. Her breasts swaying hard as she panted, her nipples had turned a dark rosy pink and her busy fingers were now in her mouth as she suckled them. Taking her clit into his mouth, Riss nipped hard at her and was rewarded with a mouth full of her juices as she screamed out his name with her release.

He loved the taste of her. The hot, sweet, honeyed taste made him want more and more of her and he continued to eat at her long after she started to beg him to stop. When his head was snapped upward, he looked at her and saw the tears on her cheeks. She had yanked him hard.

"I'm sorry, I didn't—"

"Now. I need you now." Crawling up her body, Riss nipped and kissed as much of her as he could. Taking one pert nipple in his mouth, he suckled just the tip as she wrapped her hands around his bottom and pulled him down. His hard cock slid into her just as she rolled her hips upward. Riss nearly released as soon as he rocked upward. Nothing had ever felt this good to him, and he didn't want it to ever stop.

"Come in me. Come in me, Riss, so that I can come with you." Riss nodded at her and moved in and out of her as slowly as he could. When she started scratching his back with her nails, raking them down his back until he felt blood trickle down his spine, he felt his own release coming quickly. Taking her mouth, he kissed her with all he was as the most amazing thing happened to him. His mind connected with hers in a way that he knew her every emotion, every thought, and even her need, as if they shared it too. His body released deeply into her as he threw back his head and cried out, her body tightening around him so that he knew that she'd released as well. They were one now. And he knew in that moment what Arryn had said to her was true…he loved her very much, and would for the rest of his days. Riss had found his soul mate.

Holding her in his arms, he rolled to his back, taking her with him. She fit against him in ways even his favorite blanket never did. When she lifted her head to look at him, he felt his face heat with embarrassment. He had no idea what to do now.

"You seem to be much better at this, I think. I even think you might be getting the hang of it. Have you ever had sex before me?" He shook his head. "You certainly learn fast. I don't think I've ever come so hard or so many times in my life. I think I might have to keep you."

"I enjoyed this a great deal. I have missed touching you. Seeing you when you are releasing. Your entire body seems to come alive when you do." She kissed the area over his heart, and he pulled her tighter. "You will have my child."

When she looked up at him, Riss knew that she was confused. He wanted to tell her that it was a son as well, and all about the house he'd purchased for them both, but he knew that going slowly was the only way she'd believe him. He had to make her understand a great many things and soon.

"We have been together before, as you have said. I am human when I come to you, and I impregnated you with our child. I should have thought to take care with you, but I was…it was…there was so much…."

Her laughter made him flush again, but her words had him humbled. "Yeah, I get it. We are hot when we have sex. And now that we're here again, I remember the other times with you too. And the feather." She looked up at him with a sly grin. "You have feathers."

"I do indeed." He thought she was taking this very well and rolled her to her back as he moved to the edge of the bed to stand. "Would you like to see them? I've never had a chance to show them to anyone before. Not human anyway."

At her nod, he stood up and turned his back to her. He was slightly uncomfortable with being naked now that they were no longer under the blankets, but he let his wings go and heard her breath catch. Turning slowly so as not to knock anything over, he looked at her.

"You're beautiful. I don't know really what you are, but you're the most beautiful person I've ever seen. And Riss, I'm in love with you. I think that's why this is so easy for me, the you not being a human part. I love you very much." Flushing even more, Riss shook his head at her compliment. "You are. I would love to touch you now."

When he didn't stop her, she stood up and came to stand in front of him. Her fingers dancing along his wings had his body respond in a way that made his cock harden again. When he tried to cover himself, she wrapped her hand around him.

"I will want you again if you keep this up." She moved her hand up and down him as she smoothed out his feathers. "I can feel me touching you. Not like wings, but all over my body. It's as if we're connected in a physical way. And I have changed my mind. I do want you again."

Riss lifted her up again, this time not moving to the wall but pulling her down over his thick cock and holding her there. When she tightened around him, using her body to give herself pleasure, Riss couldn't help but watch her face as she rode him.

"Riss, take me this way. Take me hard until I come all over you." He nodded and took the two steps to the wall and pressed her against it. "Hard, take me hard."

He started pounding into her even as she held onto his wings. When his climax raced over him, she screamed out his name, and he wrapped his wings around her until they were both cocooned inside. When she screamed again, her body stiffening around him, Riss nipped hard at her throat and tasted blood. Sucking hard on the wound, he felt her come again, this time pulling a few of his parts from his wings. Riss came again, filling her with his own release until he felt the world tilt on its axis. Bringing his wings back to his body, he held her until he could move again.

Staggering to the bed, he laid her down gently, then covered her up. He was going to have to explain himself to Tholan and Michael, but right now he wanted to watch her a bit more. Riss ran his fingers down her spine, then over her bottom. It was soft, yet firm, and he wanted to squeeze the firm muscles very badly. As soon as she opened her eyes and turned to look at him, he knew that leaving her was going to be the hardest thing he'd ever done.

"Don't leave me." He took her hand into his and kissed it as she continued. Sitting down beside her, he started to explain why he had to go, but she cut him off. "Please, don't go just yet. I have so many questions for you."

"I will have to leave you soon. What we have done here, what I have done here, is forbidden. I will have to pay a huge fine." She pulled him to her, and he lay beside her. Nothing they could do to him would compare to leaving her now.

"You said you're not human. And someone told me that you were a protector. Is that what this symbol is?" He looked at the emblem on his arm that had been put there by Boss so long ago. "I have a necklace that looks like it."

When she reached to the smallish night table next to the bed, he nearly kissed the exposed skin she'd shown him. But when the medallion was hovering above her breast, he reached out to touch it.

"Where did you get this?" He sat up in the bed and looked around the room, thinking that the only person who could have given this to her might be there with them. "Did Boss come to see you?"

"Yeah, he said everyone called him that. He was very nice, but I think he is a little overworked. Do you know him? Is he really your boss?" Riss nodded as the medallion swayed back and forth. He'd only seen this particular necklace once before, and it had hung on the neck of the man who she said gave it to her. If what she was saying was true, and he had no doubt that it was, then Boss was already aware of what he was doing here with Kala.

"He is my boss, yes, and I am a protector. I was sent here to watch over you. But I had decided to quit my job before I met you, and now...now I will die and leave you behind." He looked at her. "I'm so very sorry. Had I met you before, I might have...no, that's not right either. I would still have wanted to quit. I would have spent my last days with you, and it would have been worth coming to work until we had to part ways."

"What do you mean, your last days? You're saying because you're quitting being a protector that you have to die? Oh no you're not. Not now you're not. You're not dying. I won't let you." He smiled at her sadly. "No, I just found you. And if you're right about this kid, I can't raise one on my own. You tell that man you've changed your mind. You can't leave us. Or better yet, I'll tell him. You tell him to get his ass here right now, or so help me, I'll hurt him when he comes here again."

"But I must." He felt the pull of being summoned home almost as soon as he spoke. Looking at her as his body began to fade, he thought of all the things he wanted to tell her, but all he could think of now was to tell her that she was his. "I love you with all my heart, Kala Marrow, and I will miss you so very much."

She was crying for him as he left her. He could hear it even though he was pulled away. And Riss knew as surely as he was standing there alone that the sound of her cries would haunt him forever.

Chapter 9

Michael sat very still as Riss paced. He'd not said a word since he'd been brought here, but any fool could see that he was upset with them...especially him. When he finally would sit down, Riss would hop back up as if he'd been sprung from a spring only to start pacing again. When Boss entered a few minutes later, Riss dropped to his knees, and then to his chest. With his wings and arms spread wide, it looked as if the man had become a feathered rug for his master. Michael looked at Boss, and both men knew that he was in a great deal of pain.

"You disappoint me, Riss. I thought we had a deal. I never thought of you as one to break a bargain. What do you have to say for yourself? Anything?" Riss said nothing as Boss took the seat behind the big desk and continued. "You have nothing to say in your defense?"

"No. I am guilty of what you say. Please, do not punish the woman. It was all my fault. I take full responsibility." Boss looked over at him as Riss lay there talking. "I wish that you would make sure that she has the home that I have provided for her. And that—"

"You think to make deals with me? Now? After this? You think to tell me what I will do concerning a woman who has thrown herself at you countless times?" Riss did look up then when the room echoed

115

with Boss's voice. "I make the rules here, and you will do well to remember that."

"I do, sire. I do. But she didn't throw herself at me. Not like you think. I was the one who came to her. She is innocent of this matter. Please, punish me and not her." When Riss was bid to stand, he did so as he again begged for Kala's home. It was not a good thing to watch one as powerful and as strong as Riss beg for something.

"Sit." Riss sat down when commanded, and Boss looked over at him as he sat down. Michael could see the humor in his eyes. "When did you take her the shirt?"

Riss looked at him sharply, but he answered Boss. "Late last night. I came to her in a dream and gave her the information. I don't think she believed me, but she did talk to me. Along with the file of homes she was to see. I believe Arryn picked them up from her today. He was most impressed with her too."

"You took her my shirt?" Riss flushed when he looked at Boss, but he still had questions. "You had him take her my shirt and the file and didn't bother telling me about it? You do know that is what made her see me, don't you?" Riss flushed again, but he was no longer looking like a beaten man. He looked like the protector that he really was.

"I do as I please, Riss. You of all people should know that. I have my reasons for a great many things that I do not share with you. This being one that...well, I will share with you. What I can for now. And I believe it will benefit a great many people and not just you. We would like for you to marry the child, Kala Marrow. As soon as possible, as a matter of fact." Riss didn't look like he believed Boss, so Michael looked at him.

"I took her your shirt so that she could do just what she did. Boss has decided that it is time. Time for the two of you to become a couple. A couple that will do a great many things for us both here and on earth. You will both be greatly rewarded for your services." Michael handed him the file that he'd gotten from his contact on earth. "There is the house that she has chosen. As well as anything that you have desired, as well as her dreams of the things she wanted. The swing set will have to be assembled, but we are hoping you can manage that." Riss opened the file, and Michael could almost see his mind working. The man was excited, yes, but he was also very cautious. So would he be, he supposed. It was a great deal to take in. Michael looked at Boss, then at Riss. They had chosen well in this.

"Wait. I don't understand." Riss closed the file, only to open it twice more before he continued. "You want me to marry Kala, build a swing set, and set up a house with her? How long before you bring me back here to be ended from my services? Days, weeks? Will I see my child born?"

"You'll see many of them born if you do not make me regret this." Boss chuckled at his own joke. "I have decided that you are too good a protector to replace. And I will not have to if you would be so kind as to live on earth for all the time I need you, and come to me when I call. I have great plans for you, as Michael said. And in doing this for me, you'll be rewarded."

"Call me for what?" Riss had always been a man to question everything, and this didn't appear to be any different. "You'll bring me to you, here, and I'll do what for you? Watch over a child for their lifetime, only to leave my own family alone all that time? As much as I think you're a great man for giving me this

117

gift, I don't know how beneficial I can be if I know Kala and my child are all alone. I'm sorry, sir, but I don't know if I can make this work for you."

"No, you'll train new protectors." Riss sat down when Boss spoke. Even from where he sat, Michael thought Riss looked pole axed. The poor man was actually taking it better than he'd thought he would under the circumstances. "I need a good man to train them on the ways of the world, the human world. I need a man who can, even during a crisis, stand up and keep his mind on business. That is something that you cannot get from a book. There needs to be someone there, on Earth, that can be there for them and only them until they are ready to be on their own. You are that man. I'm not saying you must be with them the entire time. I would like for you to be there if they summon you, in a situation that they are not comfortable with. Understand me?"

"I think that I do. And I don't mean to question you about this, sire, but what of my life? I will not be able to keep the pace of a protector as a human. I will not be much good to you once you have released me to earth. I will become a human, will I not? I can't think that I'd be much good to you as I grew older."

Boss nodded at him, and Michael stood to answer Riss's question. "You're going to remain as an immortal. And you'll wear the crest that makes you as such. Yours that you have now will be altered to show what you've become. A new breed of protectors. Kala, too, will be branded. And all your children as well. Each of you will train and help the new protectors through time. All time." Michael handed him a medallion much like the sigil he'd given Kala, and watched as he put it on before telling him the rest. "Starting the moment that touches your skin, you will be one of the Chosen few, one of the Mystic Protectors."

Michael knew the moment that the sigil touched Riss's skin. The change between them, the connection that had always been there, changed. It morphed into something more, and he knew that his mark on his shoulder had taken on the new changes as well. Riss was now the first of the Mystics that would be his new army. He summoned Kala to come to them.

Kala appeared in the room seconds later. Riss grabbed for her when she swayed on her feet. When she was lowered gently to the chair, Boss offered her a glass of wine, which she declined. She stared at Riss, then at Boss, for long moments before she spoke. Michael was almost afraid of what she would say. He sort of liked that about her.

"I'm not dreaming." Boss shook his head and smiled at her. "This is really fucked up, you know. I don't know what's going on, but you wake me up right now. Because I know that I did not just travel through a wormhole-like thing to end up here. Where is here, anyway?"

Riss started to speak, but she glared at him and stood up to pace. They all let her. She was working up to something, and no man wanted to be in front of her when she got there. As soon as she stopped walking and turned to them again, she stood staring at Boss for several seconds.

"You came to me. Twice. You told me that I'd meet a man and his name would be Riss. I'd have to watch over him, too. You said that things would happen. I'm not sure of everything you said, but you really screwed me up." Boss nodded. "I don't like you very much right now."

"That is fine, my child. There are times when I do not care for myself, either. Please have a seat." She sat, but she didn't relax. Boss grinned at Michael before speaking. "She will be a good Mystic as well. I think I shall enjoy watching them spar with the new recruits."

"As will I." Michael turned to her. "I'm sorry about this, my dear, but it has become imperative that the man Carey be taken out. I do not mean it to be that you do so, but we will need your help in bringing him over to be dealt with."

"Don't think I didn't notice that no one answered my first question. Where am I now?" No one answered her because they could not. Michael supposed that Boss could, but He simply smiled at her. "You're not going to tell me. Is this one of those things where I wouldn't believe it even if you told me? If so, then I'm going to tell you what I told Benny. I can take a lot more truth than I can half-truths. I want it all."

"I'm sorry, love, but you are not quite ready for the full story yet. You'll learn a great deal, more than you more than likely want to know, as soon as we have taken care of Mr. Carey. It is very important that things with him settle first. Is that all right with you?" Boss leaned back in His chair as he regarded her. When she nodded, Michael felt the breath he'd not known he was holding leave his body. "You will bear a mark now, I believe. A sigil on your right arm where Riss has his."

As she pulled up her shirtsleeve, Michael looked at Riss. He was besotted with the girl. More than that, Michael knew that he loved her...would die for her, too, if it became necessary. Michael looked at Boss. At his wink, Michael felt that this plan to help the protectors might work and that these two would do them a better job than even Boss had thought they might. Things were going to be all right, Michael just knew it. And Boss was going to protect them both.

"This thing, what the fuck is it supposed to mean to me? Because if you plan on putting feathers on me, I think I'll have to pass." Michael started to tell Kala she needed to have a little more respect, but Boss held up His hand to stop him.

"And if I told you that you have them already, what would you say to that?" Boss leaned forward and looked her in the eyes as He spoke softly to her. "You are now a part of the Mystic Protectors, Kala. An elite group of men and woman who would protect humans. You were hand-picked by me to help lead them."

"You mean humans like me." Boss shook his head, and Kala nodded. They seemed to be at a standstill until Kala spoke again. "I'm no longer human because of this, am I? Somehow…maybe this mark you gave me…it's done something to me. You changed me without asking."

"I had to. You would not have survived this had I not. So no, you were no longer human the moment you became his lover. I cannot have a protector have a human as a wife. Others, the ones that would see this fail, see me fail, would have taken you and caused you a great deal of harm, even death to get to Riss. Nor would you having his child work if you were human, because the child you carry is not human. You are now and will be forevermore a Mystic." Kala started to stand but sat down hard. Boss stood up and knelt in front of her, taking her hand. "You will be all right, my child. This I promise you."

"You're not going to hurt Riss for this, are you?" Boss shook his head. "I had a feeling that because of what I did to him…to his feather, you would cause him harm. He thought he was going to die, and I thought it was because of me."

"Nay, child, it is because of me. It is something that I wanted for him...for you both. I would not kill one of my best men." Boss kissed her hand and reached for Riss's. When they were together, he kissed them both again and stood up. They were now united as a couple and no man, human or otherwise, would be able to come between them. Boss handed Riss a small box.

"It is customary for a man to give his wife a ring. I have taken the liberty of giving you both a set that will keep you safe." The rings, Michael knew, were made of the purest gold and tears. Boss had fashioned them himself, using parts of himself to form them. The rings slid on their fingers and fit them perfectly.

~~~

Dan knew that sooner or later someone was going to find out he had been at Randy's house and that someone killed him and his wife. Dan knew that he'd not done it, but the people wouldn't see it that way. He'd already seen his picture on the television as a person of interest. He had always thought of himself as uninteresting, but the news people might know more than him. But still, he'd decided he was not going to turn himself in.

Looking at his supplies, he knew that sooner or later he was going to have to go out again. The simple fact that he didn't want to didn't even come into the picture. There was only one can of food left, and it was beets. Why he'd borrowed that from Randy was beyond him.

Also, he had only three bottles of water left. He did have the five bottles of wine he'd borrowed, too, but Randy hadn't told him he would need a wine opener.

Dan was pretty sure that he'd be able to figure one out had he gotten one, but all the wine he'd ever drank had been the kind with a screw off lid. This wasn't something he was used to. He only hoped that when he and Kala moved in together, she'd not try to buy things that he didn't know how to use or open. That would make it hard for him to eat while she was at work if she did something like that to him.

"Perhaps Kala will have one." He nodded, thinking of all the times he'd picked up his phone to call her only to put it back down again. "She is with those people now. I need to get to her to tell her I'm sorry I hurt her."

He remembered hitting her but not why. Actually, he was remembering a great deal about the day at her apartment, and he knew that when he hit her, it had no doubt been her fault. Then there was the situation with his momma. Dan had to get her to agree to let them come live with her for a time, at least until Kala had a job and a place for them to live. Maybe if she could get back on with the cable company, his momma would let them stay with her. It would work out well for him if she did.

Momma was forever making him feel bad about himself, calling him names and telling him he was lazy. Kala never treated him like that. She loved him, and as soon as he got to her, they were going to get married. Dan's momma made him mad a great deal, but he'd tried his best not to hit her too often. Once when he'd been extremely mad at her, she ended up in the hospital for several days. While he had missed her a great deal, he had also realized how bossy she was.

Dan thought he knew where Kala was. There were a lot of police around the apartment building he'd been near the other day, and he'd seen enough police dramas to know that she'd be in some sort of safe house to keep her hidden away from him because of Randy and his missus. Someone had hurt them, and they might be afraid that whoever it was would hurt his Kala, too. Dan tried to think what had happened there, but all he'd been able to think was that they were both dead when he'd gotten there. And the reason blood was all over him was because he'd tried his best to save them. The person who had killed them was trying to frame him. Dan didn't know who this guy was, but he was making a mess of his life, and Dan hated it.

His train of thought was off again. When he'd been in that home, he'd been told that he had to keep track of what he was thinking. Straight thinking, they'd called it, or something like that. Dan knew that he sometimes would put too many sentences together that didn't go with what he was thinking, and people would get confused. He even confused himself sometimes. Dan had started writing notes to himself, things he wanted to make clear so that he'd have a better picture of what he wanted. Rarely did it work the way he wanted it to, but he did still try to make others pay attention to him.

"It's because I'm so smart." And he was, too. His IQ was very high. Not many people, the nurses and doctors told him, had an IQ of sixty-one and could be as smart as him. They had never been able to tell him what his roommate had as a score, but the guy had to be a five or something. He couldn't even get a girlfriend. Dan had lots of girlfriends while he'd been in the home, too many for him to remember their names right now.

Dan knew that killing things was what had gotten him put away. Never people, but animals. He had tried to tell the doctors and nurses it was because they were different from him and he'd just wanted to see what was inside of them, but they'd told him he was bad, really bad, and that he had to stop it.

"I don't want to be bad anymore. Kala won't love me if I get bad again." Dan sat down on the chair he'd found and looked around his little place. He'd come across it when he left Randy's house. He'd been really scared and had run into the first place he came across. He was glad now that he had.

It was an abandoned house that needed a lot of work. The furniture was dirty and dusty but still nice, and the walls were covered in something green, and the floors moved sometimes. He tried really hard not to think about what that could mean and spent a great deal of his time in the dining room and kitchen. The floors were hard in there and not carpeted.

There were no lights in the place, but that didn't bother him too much. The television was gone, as were all the other big appliances, like the microwave and refrigerator. He supposed his food supply was all the kind of stuff he could eat right out of the boxes, but it would have been nice to see his shows while he did.

Dan had tried to get back to his mom's house, but there was too much going on there for him to get in. He wanted his television to bring here and use. Then there were the recorders too. He knew that the cable company had turned off his free stuff, but he thought that maybe he could get something hooked up here until he figured things out. It was worth a shot. Surely they'd let him have it back in light of the fact that he didn't live with his momma right now.

His mom's house. He kept thinking about what he'd seen there...yellow tape all around the house and yard. There had been a cop car in the driveway, too, and he'd been too afraid to go there and ask them what was going on. Maybe his momma had had a heart attack or something. Dan didn't care much for her, but if she died, he'd have to go to her funeral and stuff.

Something occurred to him then.

"She'd leave me her house if she was really dead. I mean, who else is gonna want it? And it would be perfect for me and Kala. I know where everything is and all. So while she's at work, I can keep the house just like Mom did, and we'd be so happy. Cable too. Maybe she could work for the cable company again and I've have all my shows again. Yeah, that's it." Dan frowned, thinking he'd thought of this before, but it went away before he could get a good hold on the thought.

Dan pulled on his coat. It was time to get out into the world. There were things he needed to get ready, and one of them was to see what the hell had happened at his house now that he realized that his momma was dead. Kala would be so proud of him. She'd been telling him for some time that he should have a place of his own. Now he did. And the two of them would be very happy living there, too. He was smiling for the first time in a long while.

"Kala, love, when we come together, it's going to be fucking fantastic. Just like those movies I used to tell you about." The woman who stood on the street next to him looked at him. Dan had forgotten to stay focused. "Sorry, talking out loud again."

With a nod, she moved on, and he smiled at her wobbly walk. That was never going to happen to him. When he was older and not getting around well, Kala would push him everywhere he wanted to go in a fancy wheelchair. They'd be the talk of the town.

It took him over an hour to get to his house. The yellow tape had been broken in several places now and hung lazily in the yard and around the trees. Going up to the house, he didn't see anyone hanging around, so he walked to the back where he'd hidden a key long ago when his mom had locked him out. Smiling, he pulled it out from under the planter that held a now dead pansy. Going inside, he was surprised to find the electricity off.

The house was dark in the corners that still terrified him. He'd had to spend a great deal of his youth in them, standing still with his nose planted deep in the crevice. Dan remembered thinking that he'd never have a square house...all round so there would be no corners for him to have to stand in. Then when he'd gotten older, he realized that he didn't have to stand there. He was bigger. Laughing, he found the flashlight that had been in the drawer for as long as he could remember and turned it on. The shadows disappeared, and he felt a great deal better.

The house was cold, too. The heat must have been off for some time, and when he tried to turn on the television, he got a little unfocused when it wouldn't come on. He'd never understood that. When the power was off, why did it affect his television? There should be special electricity for televisions, he thought. He'd have to talk to Kala about seeing if there was a box or something he could use when this sort of thing happened.

His belly rumbled, and he turned to the kitchen. He opened the cabinets and found some of his favorite things still here. Maybe, he thought, he'd simply stay there until he found Kala. This way he could have it all fixed up for them when he talked her into coming home with him.

Going to the living room, he was surprised by the smell. Something had died in there. It took him only a few minutes to find where the smell was coming from, and he sat down across from the chair.

The blood was everywhere. And the pretty pillows that his mom crocheted were covered in spots of it, as well as the walls behind it. Dan was worried now. If his mom had had a heart attack, that was fine, but it looked to him like someone had hurt her. Running his fingers over the doilies that she'd always had on the back of her chair, he felt the stiffness of the dark stain and moved away from it.

"Momma?" He went to her bedroom, thinking that whoever hurt her would have put her in the bed to help her. The bed was still made up, and her nightgown was laying over the pillow as it had been for his entire life when she wasn't wearing it. The towels in the bath were clean too, no sign of blood anywhere. Dan went back to the living room to stare at the chair.

"I have to get rid of the chair. It'll scare Kala to have all that blood and stuff in the house. Maybe I can take it out to the burn pile." Nodding, he stood up to move it when he saw his mom's purse. He knew something really bad had happened if she left that behind. All her pills were in it.

Picking it up, he took it to the kitchen where the light was much better. There he dumped the leather thing out onto the table and looked at what she stored in it. It had always been a mystery to him how she always seemed to have whatever she wanted in that thing. Dan had secretly thought it was magical and that she would say words over it to get what she wanted. There was no way that thing held it all. Now he could see that it was just a regular bag and nothing more was in it than he'd ever seen her take out.

Her wallet had ninety dollars in it and a quarter. She'd always told him to have a quarter on him to make a call if need be. He'd tried it once, to call Kala when he'd just wanted to hear her voice, and had found out that it took three quarters to make a call. He'd meant to tell his momma that, but had never gotten around to it. Dan decided to make a note to tell her when she came home.

In addition to the money in the wallet, he found another fifty stashed deep under the lining. Smiling, he realized that his mom was something of a liar. Whenever he asked her for money, she'd told him she didn't have any. She'd lied to him a lot, he thought.

There were also three credit cards with the passwords written on them in magic marker, as well as a note attached to each of them with the balance. He wasn't sure if it was how much she owed on them or how much he could charge, but it was a lot of money. Putting them with the cash, he started opening some of the little cases inside it. Inside each of them, he found a wonderment of things, but nothing useful to him. He didn't even think Kala would want any of the things his momma had thought important enough to carry around. He thought of Kala's purse.

He'd taken it once when she'd been to lunch. Kala had some items in there that confused him a little, and still did. When he thought to ask her about them, he decided that it was probably a girl thing and forgot about them. But she did have some pictures in there of other men that he'd never liked. She was his. Dan continued looking through his momma's purse and tried not to think of Kala with other men.

In the end he'd found some change and a few pictures—none of him—and all her pills. There were also a few more cards to stores he had no idea where they were. He put everything back except what he was going to need, like the credit cards and the money. After setting it back behind her chair, he sat down again.

"Kala will have to help me with the chair. I'm not well enough for that." He wasn't really. He'd not taken his "happy pills," as his mom called them, in days, and now he was starting to feel less than happy. "Once Kala comes to be my wife, I'll be happy all the time. She will make sure that I'm happy all the time. It will be her job."

Going to his room, he stood staring at it for some time before he finally went in. Someone had robbed him, and had made a horrible mess of things. His momma was going to blame him for this and he'd be in a lot of trouble again.

All his pictures of him and Kala were gone. The things she'd given him, too, were no longer hanging in the closet next to his things. Even her panties and bras, the ones he'd found in her laundry basket when he'd gone there for a visit, were gone. But it was his wall to her that disturbed him the most. All the lists of things she'd said to him, the sticky notes she'd left him, and the ones where she told him she loved him were also gone. Dan went to the wall to see if maybe they had fallen off, but there was nothing there. None of his things that they had shared were there. All his wonderful memories of Kala and him were gone, and he felt his anger bubbling out.

"Why would someone take my things?" He opened his drawers and found even his clothes had been mussed up, moved around, and not in the neat way he'd liked them. "Momma will be so mad when she sees this, and I'm not going to take the blame for this. No siree. I'm not at fault this time. Someone is going to have to come here and bring me back my things and straighten this stuff up. Or there will be hell to pay." Dan felt his anger take him over, a rage that seemed to consume him, and he let it take him. He needed this.

He tore through the room, tossing emptied drawers to the floor, knocking over his dresser and desk, to find anything that had been theirs. Finally, when he'd dropped to the floor, he saw a small sticky that had been missed and held it to his nose. It still smelled of her. His Kala.

The smiley face was smudged, but he could still make it out. She'd given it to him when he'd been off. He'd told everyone that he'd been sick, but he hadn't. There had been a marathon of his favorite show, and he wanted to watch them all over before the new season premiered. Kala had told him he shouldn't do things like that, but had given him the sticky already and hadn't asked for it back. Dan thought that that's when she finally fell in love with him...the moment she'd tried to help him to be a much better man.

Dan lay down on his ruined bed, holding the note to his heart. He would have to find her now instead of waiting for her to come to him. The house was a mess, and he needed to watch his shows. They always calmed him. Dan decided as he closed his eyes that he was going to have to go to the police and find out what had happened to his wife and mother. Kala should have been home by now, and he had no idea where his mother had gotten herself off to. Dan needed to find his family, and soon.

Chapter 10

"I guess we're married." Riss nodded, but didn't move from the chair he'd sat in when they came home. They'd been brought back to the safe-house apartment a few minutes ago, and now she seemed to be nervous with him there. "Does this happen often? Where someone—I guess a human—is transported to wherever we were from here?"

"Not often, but it happens sometimes. I guess he thought that since you were no longer human it would be all right." Riss wanted to go to her and hold her, but she seemed so fragile right now. "Would you like to talk about what Boss said?"

"Not yet." She moved through the room touching things or picking them up, only to set them back down with a small adjustment to it. When she finally sat down across from him, he could tell that she was going to say something, but he was pretty sure he didn't want to hear it. So he decided to tell her something about himself.

"I've been a protector since I was created. That was when things were a little less busy and there were not nearly the amount of people there are now. It's been a long and sometimes scary thing to protect present-day humans compared to the ones when we first began. I've been to several wars on the front line, too, most of which I never understood, but I had a job to do. And not all of the things I've been sent to protect have been humans." She nodded and leaned back, and he felt himself relax a bit. "I've watched over several other creatures. A few worms, too."

Riss shivered, and she laughed. "I take it that wasn't one of your more favorite jobs? And how long does a worm live anyway?"

"Six long and very boring years." He smiled when she laughed again. "They are very productive in a sort of odd way. They poop a great deal and burrow. And when they do that, they help turn the earth for water and other nutrients to get into the soil. Even when they poop, they leave behind fertilizer and other things."

Riss was quite proud of his knowledge of his charge. He'd had a great deal of time to think while watching over them. When Kala stood up and walked behind him, he put his hands on hers when she touched his shoulders.

"I'm afraid of messing up." Before he could tell her that she was going to be fine, she kissed him. The position, with her standing behind him like this, was oddly erotic. Her hands moved down his chest to his waist as she leaned over him until her breasts were at his mouth. Riss felt his cock harden. He wanted her to touch him, but he knew that she was in charge at the moment. Her fingers sliding into the top of his pants caught his breath.

"You are very good at making me aroused." She kissed his throat, and Riss lost all train of thought. She was going to kill him in ways no one else had been able to. Kala brushed her fingers over the tip of his cock, and he rocked upward. "Kala, love, I need you."

"I'm going to take you in my mouth this way." He moaned when she opened his pants, but her next words had him reaching for her. "You can eat me this way, too. We can pleasure each other at the same time. I know we need to talk, but right now I need this. More than just sex, I need to connect with you physically. All right?"

Moving his hands up her waist to her hips, he found the drawstring on her pants, undid it, and pulled them down as far as he could. When his hands were filled with her hot flesh, he adjusted her so that her womanhood was near his mouth. Kala spread her thighs for him, and he pulled her over his mouth and suckled at her femininity.

Her moans only made him want more. Every time she made a small noise, he tried something different. He wanted her pleasure as much as his own. And then suddenly he couldn't breathe. She had not just taken him into her mouth, but was fisting him at the same time. Riss knew that if he didn't release soon, it would be a small miracle. Going back to her, he bit down on her gently and was rewarded with a flood of her cream as she reached her peak.

Cupping her bottom, he pulled her tighter to him. He wanted more, wanted to give her more. Her body was his now, forever and ever, and he was going to enjoy it as much as he could. As soon as he felt his own release coming over him, Riss slid his tongue deep within her and slid his fingers along her hard nubbin. When she came again, bowing up off him, Riss reached for his cock.

He was wet with her saliva so much so that he was able to slide his hand up and down quickly. His cum jettisoned from him, and he cried out with each stream of it. Kala took him into her mouth again, and Riss saw stars as he released again, his body aching with it. They would never live long if they kept this up, but he thought it was a perfect way to end one's life...cradled between the thighs of the woman he loved.

Her body was lax over his when they both settled. Moving her around, he pulled her into his arms and held her, cocooned her into his arms. She had long since shed the rest of her clothes, and Riss found he wasn't embarrassed, as he thought he would be, but was comforted in the thought of having her so close to him.

"I've never done that before." He started to tell her he hadn't either when she continued. "Someday I'd like to tie you to my bed and go over every inch of you with my mouth."

Riss felt his cock stir, and his mind started racing. "I could tie you to a bed? You'd enjoy that?"

"Oh yes." She turned in his arms so that she was straddled over his lap now. His cock was thickening now, and he cupped her breast to bring the tip to his mouth. Her rocking forward motion brought him to his full length, and he wanted her again. Her voice was thick with something, and he thought it was her need again. "You can use scarves or ties. You have a lot of ties, don't you?"

"I do. I had been trained to dress well when we started out. What kind of bed would you need to do this?" His mind was going over each possibility of how to get this accomplished. To have her at his mercy sounded enjoyable for them both. "Would you have to have a special one?"

"No, just an ordinary bed." She shifted again and he rolled his hips upward. "You should know that if you keep this up, I'm going to ride you like a bull and come all over you again."

"I love it when you do that." This was getting more and more intriguing, and he wanted to explore each adventure with her now and decided to tell her. "Do you have any idea how much I want to do all kinds of things with you? And to you?"

When Kala sat up on her knees and asked him to hold his cock, he did so without hesitation. Her body lowering over his took him deep, and he had to hold her hips still when she was sitting on him again. But now he was deep within her, and he could touch her in ways he'd not been able to before.

"Oh my, this is wonderful." He took her breast into his mouth and suckled it, then did the same for the other. "Oh yes, I love this riding thing."

When her hips began to rotate over his, Riss nearly passed out. Nothing had prepared him for this. Her body was a fluid motion of water, moving to her own music that only she could hear. Putting his hands on her hips, he held her to him tightly when she rocked forward and helped her roll back to start over. Riss pulled her mouth to his and kissed her as his own release built again.

"I will come in you this way. Deeper than I've ever been." He moaned when she started moving faster. "Yes, that's it. Ride me, Kala. Take your pleasure from me."

Her movement became quick jabs, her breath hot puffs of air that seemed to scorch his face. Every time she moved back and forward again, Riss watched her face. She wasn't pretty, not even lovely, but simply beautiful. Cupping her ass to bring her femininity hard against his groin, Riss watched her as she came, her body becoming hard as it bowed back, her scream of release music to his ears. And when his own release took him, he was amazed at the strength of it, the way it seemed to come from his entire body to fill her. And when she dropped her head on his shoulder, Riss rolled her to her back on the couch and pounded into her again and again until he had a second, then a third release. Body spent, he fell atop her.

"You have broken me." Her giggle had him lifting his head to stare down at her. "I love you, Kala Marrow. So very much. I don't know what I would have done had I not found you when I did."

"I love you, too. I know it seems really fast, at least it does to me, but it also feels perfect. Like we were meant to be together from the beginning of time." He nodded, knowing just how she felt. "What's your last name anyway?"

"I have none." He kissed her cheek and was making his way to her mouth when she pulled his head up. "We have no need for them where I come from. I suppose we could make one up...you could. I'm not sure what I would call myself."

"What do others of your kind do when they come here?" He wasn't sure if he could tell her she knew of a few others like himself, but felt Michael touch his mind.

"*You will have to tell her sooner or later. The man will be a large part of both your lives.*" Michael laughed. "*If I were you, however, I would introduce him to her with a little more clothing on. Oh, and I have taken the liberty of sending your things as well as hers to your home. Everything there has been taken care of as you wished.*"

Riss sat up, suddenly embarrassed. "*Please refrain from looking down on us when we are together as such.*" Michael laughed and promised he would get a bell for any future conversations.

Riss sat up, pulling Kala with him. He tried to think how to tell her, but thought that Michael may be right. Getting dressed might make his desire to have her again lessen. When she stood up, he decided there was not enough clothing in the world to do that, and followed her to the bedroom. They really did need to talk.

"Love? I would like to tell you what we are and what our child will be." She nodded and sat down on the edge of the bed. "But first, I'd like to introduce you to a good friend of mine and her husband. You know him, but not her. Her name is Lilith, and she was a protector like me."

Riss dressed as he did every day as he spoke. Wishing himself dressed in the right things had become second nature to him, and he never thought to tell her she could do the same until she was dressed herself. It was long into the night before he finished, and he was reasonably sure she was overwhelmed to the point of shutting down. When she finally spoke, he smiled. She was going to be just fine.

"I think we should see this house you bought first. Then I'd like to see how to use these wings. Okay?" Nodding, he pulled her into his arms. Yes, they were going to be just fine.

~~~

Dan was slowly running out of food. Well, not really slowly, he thought with a frown, just running out of things he knew how to cook. There were all sorts of things in the cabinets, but nothing he knew a thing about. Like, why were there four bags of flour? And three of sugar? Not to mention there were cans of things like peas and asparagus that he didn't even like when his mother cooked them. This was completely unfair.

Picking up the phone again, he slammed it down in the cradle. The phone wasn't working again. Twice now he'd tried to use it and there was nothing there.

Finally, he had to go and get his phone off the charger. It, too, was dead.

"Why is this happening to me?" Sitting down at the table, he could feel the tears threaten. He had only needed a little electricity to charge his phone. Surely there was that much still in the lines. Dan knew that once they shut off the water, there was still water in the pipes. Why wasn't there some in the electrical lines as well?

He had to find a way to get in touch with Kala. Things were going from bad to worse, and his head was hurting again. Smacking himself several times to try to knock the pain free, he laid his head on the hard surface and closed his eyes to think.

"She has to come home." Kala was going to have so much to catch up on when she finally came to him. "The laundry is piling up. I need my room cleaned up, too. And I want to watch my shows. She'll need to go to the store and pay the bills. It's a good thing she has money saved. I think she's going to need it when she finally gets here."

Dan had tried to clean up his room a little when he'd woken up that morning. But it was simply too much. There were broken pieces of his dresser all over the place, his pillows were torn to shreds, and even his clothes were all torn up and messy. His mother would have a fit if she could see this place. He raised his head when he heard someone knock on the front door.

Earlier someone had come to the door, and he nearly opened it hoping to find Kala, but at the last second he looked out the small peep hole and saw the cop standing there. Dan knew that he'd wanted to talk to one of them before, but at that moment he couldn't for the life of him remember what it had been about. So he'd stood frozen in fear of what the officer might want from him until he left. That had been over two hours ago. Dan moved to the door as quietly as he could to see if anyone stood there now.

It was another cop. This one was a woman and she had her hand on her gun like she meant business. Dan didn't open the door this time either, but waited for her to either come in (which he supposed was possible since he'd just realized he forgot to lock the door) or go away. He really hoped she'd just go away until his head felt better. Dan didn't do well when his head pained him like this.

"Mr. Carey? Are you in there?" Dan wasn't sure her knowing his name was a good thing but kept his mouth shut. "Mr. Carey? I need for you to come down to the station with me. There's a few questions we want to ask you about your mother's murder."

Murder? Before he could think not to, Dan tore open the door and jerked the cop inside with him. She was sputtering at him when he slammed her against the wall and put his hand over her mouth.

"My momma is dead?" She nodded, and when he felt her hand move he removed his hand from her mouth, grabbed both her wrists, and jerked them up over her head and held them there. That's when he noticed she had her gun in one hand. "Drop it or one of us might get hurt. I don't want that, do you? Please, just drop it on the floor and I'll do what you want."

She didn't do as he told her, and Dan was suddenly afraid. He just knew that she'd killed his momma and had taken his Kala away, too. He'd reason with her, he thought. Ask her where his Kala and Momma were, and if she didn't know, see if she could help him find them. The gun was only out to protect herself from him, and he wanted to assure her that he was harmless, that he'd learned his lesson a long time ago.

When he stepped back from her, he watched as she dropped to the floor. Dan took several steps back again until he felt the couch bump him in the back of the knees. Someone had killed her. Shot her to death. Sitting down, he stared at the blood as it pooled beneath her and stained the carpet. His momma was really going to be upset when she came in to see this. Then Dan remembered that she was murdered.

"Who killed her, do you know?" The body didn't offer up any suggestions, and Dan started to cry. Whoever was killing these people was trying to make it so he never got answers. These people were watching him and waiting until he was nearly ready to have something, some little titbit of information before they snatched it away. Dan whimpered when someone spoke loudly near the woman.

It took him several minutes to realize she was wearing a two way. Someone by the name of Anderson was trying to reach her, and he kept saying her name. Officer McKay didn't answer him, and Dan was about to tell him someone had murdered her like they had his momma when Anderson said his name.

"Carey? We know she was coming to see you today. If you can hear this, then pick up the mike and speak to me." Dan shook his head as the man continued. "There are cops all around the place. If you've harmed McKay, then there will be no place for you to hide because I will find you. Just pick up the mike, or give it to McKay so she can tell me she's all right. Please?"

"I didn't do anything to her. She just got murdered by someone and it wasn't me." He realized the man couldn't hear him but continued anyway. "What the hell am I supposed to do? Tell me. All these things are happening to me, and I don't know how to make them stop. I'm afraid for Kala. Will they hurt my wife if I go near her?"

Kala was the most important thing to him right now. He needed her, more than he ever had his momma. And the house needed to be cleaned now, as well as food cooked for him. Kala, he knew, was the only person who could do that for him. And she was gone to somewhere he didn't know. Dan wanted this to end now.

Dan started to pace around the room when he looked down at his body. Everything he had on was sprayed with a fine mist of red spots. It took him several seconds to realize it was from Officer McKay. He was covered in her blood. It was happening again. Someone was trying to frame him for another murder.

Going to the bathroom, he looked in the mirror, and all he could see were his eyes shining back at him. At first it startled him, because he didn't even recognize himself, but when he leaned in, Dan was shocked at how he looked.

His hair was mussed up, so he tried fixing it with his fingers. Turning on the tap resulted in nothing, so he began looking around for something, anything that would help him. Finding a brush buried at the bottom of one of the darkened drawers, he ran it though his hair and brought it to some order.

His face was covered in the blood, too, and scrubbing at it only made it worse. Dan was beginning to feel like he was stained now. That the person who had killed the officer was making sure that everyone thought it was him. Dan went to the officer's body again and listened to Anderson try to get her to answer him. Dan knew it was time to leave.

A long time ago, he'd been locked in the basement. His momma had said it was for his own good, but he'd never understood that. She'd given him all his food through the basement window outside, and he'd given her back the dishes the same way. And if he didn't do as he was told, she'd hold his food from him until he did. Dan had escaped twice before she figured out how he was getting out. While she'd never put him down there again, he had gone to great links to make sure if she ever did, he could still get out. Going to the basement, he closed the door behind him and set the lock. Hurrying down the stairs, he thought of something his momma had told him.

She'd told him that he'd killed his father. But Dan knew that wasn't true. As far as he could remember, it had only been him and his momma. She'd taken care of him when he was little. And then when he got bigger, he'd taken care of her. Of course, she still had to keep the house and cook, but he gave her use of his free cable.

The dankness of this part of the house had always scared him. His momma had told him that she'd buried him down there because she needed his pension check. Dan had never doubted that she had. He had wondered how she thought he'd killed him, but had never asked her. She seemed to be really upset when he asked about how people died. Going to the far wall, he moved the large cabinet out of his way and opened the smallish door behind it. Picking up the other flashlight that he'd put there, he made sure it worked before he closed himself in.

He had no idea why the little doorway had been put in here. His mom hadn't told him, and he'd never been able to ask anyone else. He supposed that was good, because now that nobody knew, he could get away from whoever was killing those people. Pulling the door closed, he reached up to the chain that was hanging there and pulled it until he heard the cabinet move back into place. He heard a loud crash just as the small hallway got completely dark. Dan thought maybe the police were in his house.

Dan followed the small, dirty hall. He'd had to stop twice and go back because he'd gotten turned around, and all the bread crumbs he'd left for him to follow long ago were gone. He knew it was the killer. The man was trying to mess him up at every turn.

"Not anymore." Dan's voice echoed along the empty hall, and it scared him enough that he stopped and turned off the light. He didn't want to get caught down there, and he certainly didn't want to be murdered there either. "Kala would be heartbroken if she couldn't see me one more time."

Nodding to himself that he was okay, he started on his way again until he saw the small beam of light at the end. Smiling, he nearly started running to it but was afraid that the murderer was trying to trap him again, so he began to watch for traps. It wasn't until he pushed the small door open that he felt better. He moved into the neighbor's garage and closed the door behind him as quietly as he could. Dan was safe. For now.

Going to the ladder that had hung there since he was a kid, Dan used it to get into the attic part of the garage. Up there was where he'd hidden a backpack, and he pulled it down. Putting the ladder back from where he'd gotten it, Dan went to the door and noticed the new car sitting where there had always been a very old and dirty one. He had no idea why he'd not noticed it before, but now that he could see the shininess of it, he wanted to drive it. Going over to it, he wondered if they'd care if he borrowed it for a few hours.

Dan started to the house when he saw that the police were all over his yard. He ducked back into the garage before anyone saw him. Getting in the car, he tossed his pack in the back. Now he had to find the keys. Smiling, he remembered something from one of his shows. Pulling down the visor, the keys fell in his lap. Pressing the garage door opener that hung where the keys had been, he pulled out of the door and drove in the opposite direction of his house. Dan turned on the radio and started singing to the tunes. He was home free.

Chapter 11

Kala wasn't sure what to think of the house. They'd come here late last night just after the news broke that Dan had murdered a cop, and she'd not had a chance to look around. Now she sat in the dining room and tried to get her pounding heartbeat under control. This was just too much.

She looked up when Lily sat down across from her. Kala had met her just an hour ago and had come in here to get away from them all. Lily's smile did nothing to make her feel better. Kala started to ask her to go away, but she spoke first.

"It's too much, isn't it?" Kala nodded. "I thought so. But I have to tell you, you're doing better than Benny did the first time he met all of them. He freaked out and had to be locked away for a time."

"I most certainly did not." Benny sat down next to his wife and kissed her on the cheek. He pushed a glass of water at her. "Drink this and I'll tell you what's going on. Unless you'd rather talk about Carey."

"I don't think so." She knew that Benny had told Riss and Michael, but she had walked away when he started talking. "I guess you're a protector too."

"No, Lily is. She mostly teaches at the college, but she helps them out when they need her to." Benny looked at his wife with so much love as he continued.

147

"She was my protector before I met her. She'd been assigned to me from about my teenage years on, and knew what I was to her for years. It wasn't until Michael came to me that I saw her. After that it wasn't all roses and chocolates."

"You didn't like her?" Kala found that hard to believe, looking at them now. "I think I loved Riss from the moment I saw him."

Kala felt her face heat up when Benny winked at her. She supposed they all knew what had happened with her and that fucking feather. She was going to have a little up close and personal time when she saw Boss again. He shouldn't be telling stuff like that.

"Have you looked over the book they gave you?" Kala nodded at Lily's question. "If you have any problems with the more personal stuff, just let me know. I can come here anytime you want. This house, like all of the protector homes, is warded so that we can be safe here."

"All of you? How many of you are there?" Lily looked at her husband, who got up to leave. Kala was slightly embarrassed to have blurted out the question, but when Lily smiled at her, Kala smiled back.

"No one knows really. You and Riss are the first couple that I've been told about and met. But over the decades I've seen a few that I heard about. We mostly keep to ourselves for some reason unless there's a mate." Lily leaned back in the chair and smiled. "You're going to have a child."

"Yes." Kala blushed again. "I guess Riss can even tell the exact date he'll be born. I don't want to know yet."

"You can too if you want. I'll show you when you're ready. You can do all sorts of things now that you're a protector. Or I should say a Mystic. You and

Riss are going to be extremely busy, I think, once this gets off the ground." Kala nodded. "Did anyone say when the field would be complete?"

Michael had taken her and Riss out to a large, wooded area earlier that morning where men and women were working, cutting down trees and other shrubbery. He told them that a large building would be put up and the grounds modified to accommodate the walking tracks and the basketball courts. It was to keep the new Mystic and Protectors in shape.

"I heard next week. Is that even possible?" Lily laughed and told her that a great many things were possible when they had the Boss helping out. "Do you like him? Boss, I mean? He seems a little...I don't know. I was going to say exhausted all the time but I think it's more than that."

"He is. When I was with Him last, I noticed it, too. But since you and Riss have come together, I've noticed a change in Him. He seems to be happier. Did you know that He has six more sets of wedding bands? Benny asked Him who was getting them, and He said that time would tell. By the way, that's His answer for everything when He wants to be all secretive. Boss is very good at that, too."

Kala nodded and thought about what she wanted to ask Lily before she made a fool of herself. "I don't know how to be what they want. Will they take all this away from us if I fail? I don't...I'm not like you guys."

"But you are." Kala started to shake her head, and Lily took her hand. "You are, Kala. Just like all of us. Come on. Let me show you something."

They went through the kitchen and out to the backyard. Every time Kala came out here she wanted to kick off her shoes and run barefooted through the grass, her grass. When Lily smiled at her again, Kala had a feeling she knew just what she was thinking and felt her face heat again. There didn't seem to be any secrets between any of them, and Kala was having a hard time with that. She had kept to herself for the better part of her life, and now there were so many people around her all the time it sort of frightened her. She looked at Lily when she cleared her throat.

"Okay, I want you to close your eyes and think about a bird." Kala looked at her and tried to think what the hell she was talking about. "Just trust me. Think of a bird. Any bird will do for this."

When she did as she was asked, a falcon popped into her mind. She had no idea where that came from and nearly opened her eyes when Lily laughed. It was a bird but a big frigging one.

"No, don't open your eyes just yet. This is going to work, you'll see. I want you to think of her feathers, the softness of them, and the way they seem to spread open when she's in flight. Are you seeing her?" Kala told her she was and was surprised at how detailed the image was becoming. "Good girl, now think of her talons, the sharp points and the long slender legs. The way she looks when she's sitting on a branch. Think of anything and everything you can about her."

The harder she thought of the bird the more details came to her. Soon she could see her flying in the sky, a dark spot so high up. When Lily asked her to open her eyes, Kala looked at her and Riss, who was now standing beside her. Kala started to take a step forward but felt...odd.

"Riss?" He came to her instead and took her hands. He was looking at her strangely, and she thought something had happened. "What's wrong? Dan hasn't come here, has he?"

"No, love. You've done it." She frowned at him, not sure what he meant. "Your wings, they've come out to play. I knew that if you didn't think about it they'd appear. You're the most beautiful creature I've ever seen. Look at them."

Turning just a little, she could see them. They were large and full, as white as the clouds above, and looked to be as soft as a baby's skin. She pulled her hand from his and touched the upper ward curve of her right wing and realized she could feel it through her body. Kala looked at Riss.

"I have wings." He laughed when she did and nodded. "What the hell am I supposed to do now? Can I fly?"

"Whatever you like. As of right now, you've taken the steps necessary to be a Mystic. Having your wings will open all the other things you can do. As well as your immortality." He kissed her mouth and pulled back slightly. "I wish we were alone. I've been practicing with my ties, and I think I have a knot that will keep you safe and secured to our bed so that I can explore every inch of you."

Kala felt her knees tremble and her body react to him. Looking around him, she saw that at some point Lily had gone and now it was just the two of them in the open field. Moving her hand down his chest to his cock, she cupped him in her hand and held him. He moaned as he rocked forward.

"I thought I was going to go first." He shook his head and leaned into her throat. She loved it when he nipped at her, and she wanted to pull him down so she could do that same to him. When he growled low, she wrapped her free arm around his waist and held him for support.

"I'm going to enjoy taking you when they're all gone. I plan to strip you naked and touch parts of you that I've missed. I think there is a great deal more of you to lick and kiss that you denied me the other day." She doubted he'd missed anything of her, but before she could say it, he continued. "When I'm finished with your body, I plan to take you hard and fast while you're still tied down. I want to be able to release inside of you without you touching me. You distract me from my purpose."

"There are people in the house, and I think they've overstayed their welcome." His laughter seemed to skim along her skin. "Seriously, I think you should tell them that we've had enough today and need some quiet time. Some really quiet time on the bed. Can you do that?"

"Or we could do this." She felt him wrap his wings around her and felt cocooned by it. Then when he opened them again, they were in their bedroom. Riss picked her up and laid her gently on the bed.

"What about the rest of them? Won't they wonder what the hell happened to us when they go outside to get us?" He told her they had to get their own wives. "Really, Riss, we can't just come up here and have sex because—"

Her mouth watered when he ran his hands down his chest and his shirt disappeared. Then when he touched his pants, they, too, were gone, and he stood before her in a pair of silky boxers and nothing else. She could see that he was hard, and there was a small stain on the front where his cock was. Kala decided that she could care less what the rest of them did, and as far as she was concerned, she had all she needed right there.

"Spread your arms and legs for me." Nodding, she did as he asked. "I'm not going to harm you. You know that, correct?"

"I know." She watched him as he moved to her arms and tied a bright blue tie around her wrist. "You do know that this is going to ruin them, don't you? You have some really pretty ties. Are you sure you want to do this?"

"Oh yes." When her left arm was secure, he moved to her left ankle. "And I have thousands of ties, and if it takes us lifetimes to ruin them, I will simply purchase more of them."

When he had her tied to the bed, she looked at him. He was looking at her as if she were a feast and he was going to gorge himself. As soon as he put his first knee on the bed and started up her body, Kala felt her pussy soak.

"Riss, I'm not going to last long. And with all my clothes on, you're not going to enjoy this as much as I am." He put his hand on her pant leg, and she felt his bare touch. Looking down, she saw that her pants were gone and she was laying there in her panties. "You can do that to me, too?"

"You can as well. Strip me naked and yourself with just a touch." He would tell her this after he tied her up when there was no way for her to test out this new thing. "Do you want me to let you go?"

"Yes. No." He grinned as he touched her pussy. "Riss, please? You're killing me. Just let me come and I'll be able to take more of your play."

"Oh, I will play. I have a lovely body here to explore. And I plan to take all the time I can with you."

That's what she was afraid of.

~~~

Tasting her as he licked along her thigh, Riss could feel her muscles move under his tongue. Every quiver of her skin made him want to do more to her. And her scent was almost more than he could bare. Licking along the top of her panties, Riss heard her begging him again and slid his finger under the elastic and along her gate. She nearly bucked him off when he buried his nose in her wet heat.

"Come for me, Kala. I would love to taste you as you do." Her body reacted to his request by doing just as he'd asked her to do. He touched the silk and removed it as he lapped hungrily at her. When she came a second, then a third time, Riss sat up. It was time to get serious about exploring her. Moving to the end of the bed, he touched his fingers gently to her ankle and started telling her what he was finding.

"Do you have any idea how lovely your ankles are? This one I love the most because of the art you've had put here." He kissed the small angel and moved his mouth over her tiny toes. "And these little gems are so beautiful. The way you paint them bright red, yet hide them away so that no one but you and I know what you've done. Why do you do that?" He didn't expect an answer so wasn't really surprised when she didn't give him one. But moving up to her calf had him pause. He loved a woman's legs, and these were exceptional.

"I've watched women walk before and wondered how they did it. Their hips swing back and forth, feet in small shoes with such high heels." He kissed the back of her leg and then licked a path up to the back of her knee. "But you've got walking down to perfection. The way your body seems to have mastered it long before any other person has. It moves and sways like it's a form of art. And it's all mine now."

Her knee held a special interest to him because he found a small scar there. Running his finger over the long-ago wound, he was surprised at how badly he wanted to go and find the reason it was there and harm someone for it. But when he ran his tongue over the wound, he discovered that she'd done it herself falling from an apple tree.

"You should take better care of yourself from now on. I would hate to have to see you hurt. Even if it is just a little." Riss moved to her other ankle and toes and gave them the same treatment. By the time he was to the tiny little tattoo on her outer calf, he was as hungry for her as he'd ever been for anything before.

"What have you here?" The small bird looked to be something he'd seen before but couldn't think. He supposed it had something to do with his view that was distracting him as well. He had taken her panties off, and now he could see how wet and gorgeous she really was. The bird was forgotten for the moment, and he ran his fingers up both her thighs to her hips.

"Riss? Please?" Her voice was soft yet so powerful he could feel the need in it. Touching the downy fur over her femininity, he watched her face as he slid down into her opening with his fingers.

"You're not making this easy on me." She moaned as he moved his fingers in and out of her, and he, too, moaned when she tightened around him. "Would you like to come again, love? I could drink from you while you did so."

"Riss, you either fuck me or let me go so I can fuck you." He nearly laughed, but she pulled tight on the bounds that held her. "Give your cock to me."

He moved up her body, fisting his cock as he went. He would do this again to her, hold her down while he finished his study. But when his cock was at her entrance, all he could think about was burying himself as deep as he could into her and staying there for the rest of their lives.

She nearly pulled him in with her need. Her hips rolled up and down so much that he could have stilled above her as he was and released. Moving slowly into her, inch by inch, Riss knew that the moment that she released, he would join her. But when he was buried to the root of himself, she stilled beneath him.

"Riss, I love you." He kissed her, drinking more of her into him with his mouth and tongue. "Please never leave me."

Reaching up to release her arms, they wrapped around him even as he touched his foot to the ones around her ankles. When she was completely surrounding him, he started to move harder and faster as he kissed her again.

"Never. I'll never leave you. I love you more than my life. I would die for you. I would kill for you. I love you with all my heart." When she came screaming his name, Riss followed her. There was no better thing in the world, he discovered, than to make love to your wife and have her love you right back.

It was perhaps an hour later when he heard from Michael, who asked for him to come to the kitchen. Riss had been watching Kala sleep since they'd made love, and he was debating whether or not to do as Michael asked. Riss told him he'd be down in a few moments after debating on telling him to go away.

"We have a location on Daniel. And now that we know where he is, I've told him to come here so that this might end peacefully. He is driving his car on the way to here." Riss sat down when given this news as soon as he walked into the room. Michael handed him a small map, and Riss looked at it as Michael continued. "He will be here within the hour. This is the route that he's taking. I know that it's the longer way around, but that's what I had hoped for. This way we can prepare better for him when he gets here. I've also contacted Benny and Lily, and they will be here as well."

"Do you honestly think this will end peacefully?" Riss looked up at him when he didn't answer. "He wants her, and I cannot think that he will say it's all right once he realizes that she isn't going to go with him. He will, I think, be most upset with her. And me as well."

"It will end as it should. I know that's not what you want to hear from me right now, but it's all I can offer you. This is where it will end. When he arrives, it will be over almost before it begins. We need to stop this. And the only way is to help the police." Michael sat down when he finished, and Riss thought he looked tired. There seemed to be a great deal of that going around, and Riss was worried. Benny sat beside him when he came into the room.

"I have my best men around the house, as well as a few snipers in the trees. I would like him to be taken alive per Boss's instructions, but if it comes down to it, we'll do this whatever way we need to. First and foremost, we need to keep the other humans here safe." Riss nodded at Benny. There was no way that Riss could think that this was going to end well for anyone.

Riss knew that as of today there were nine humans in his household. Some of them were going to stay after this was over, as security, and few of them would know who they were protecting. But Benny had brought in his men and women to pretend to be a part of the household and keep the staff safe.

"Kala is resting. She has her wings now, and her sigil is there. She will be safe." Michael nodded at him. "Will the babe...will it be all right if things get bad?"

"It will. I would never ask her to help with this if there was the slightest chance of anything happening to her or the baby she carries. It will be the first child born to one of our kind. We are to keep him safe above everything. And in turn, his mother and father." Riss nodded at Michael.

"What do you want me to do?" They all looked up at Kala when she walked into the room. "I'm not going to sit by and let him hurt anyone else. You wouldn't like me if you even tried." Riss knew this. She was nothing if not loyal to her friends, and he knew that even through all this, she still thought of Dan as the man he'd been, not what he'd become.

"No one would try," Michael told her. She came to him when Riss put out his hand. "You're ready to listen now? The plan is very simple."

Michael handed her what looked like a small cell phone, but it was really a recorder. They didn't want anyone to think that she'd trapped him into confessing what he'd done, and recording it was the best solution. This had been Benny's idea, and it sounded like a good one. As she got instructions once again on what to do, Riss watched the woman who meant the world to him, and felt his love for her expand.

"I will keep her safe for you." Riss knew that He would and told Boss so. *"You and I will need to talk once this is over. I have some things...a few things that I would speak to you about with this course I have selected for you."*

"You mean finding Kala for me, or the plans you have for some of the other protectors?" Boss laughed and said both. *"I had thought that's what you'd want. Do you have*

any idea…well, I'm sure you do know, but will I know who you have plans for next?"

"No, not until it is time for you to. It is more fun to watch it unfold, much like a train accident that you mustn't watch but find that you cannot look away from." His laughter rang in his head, and Riss asked Him if He was coming there. *"No. It is best that I do not. It hurts me in ways you cannot know to watch one such as Daniel to be like this. He'll be…well, he will get all the help he needs now and after. He is going to need it."*

Riss hoped so. The man was going to go away for a very long time, and in that time he would need a great deal of help. After the connection to Boss and himself closed, Riss went outside. It was time.

Chapter 12

Dan pulled into the driveway and looked around. The yard was bigger than his neighborhood, and the house was as big as the courthouse. He wondered again why this house seemed to be calling to him. But here he was. Looking in the mirror, he could see that his stop just down the road had done him a world of good. Dan ran his fingers through his hair again just to make sure. Getting out of the car, he stood by it and took several deep breaths before turning to the house again. It appeared much bigger now that he was out of his car.

His wife was in there. Kala was finally going to come to him, and he was more than ready. The house that he had lived in as a child would no longer due, of course. He could see that now. And he also knew that he'd have to behave, too. No more letting his medications slide, and he'd also have to control his eating. He noticed that the pants he'd pulled on in the gas station had been a little snug. There were other things, too. Things he'd have to do to make sure she was never hurt again. The persons who were trying to frame him would not go unpunished either.

"No matter, no matter. She'll whip me into shape." Dan started for the house when the front door opened and a man stepped out. Dan didn't move for several seconds as he tried to remember if he knew him or not.

When the man smiled at him, Dan moved forward with the intentions of introducing himself. But the man spoke first.

"Daniel Carey?" Dan nodded. "I've been waiting for you. Would you like to come in?"

Dan felt his mind scream at him that this was a trap. So instead of moving toward the door, Dan stopped at the bottom of the stairs. He didn't even reach for the man's hand when he put it out for him to shake. Not that he was afraid of him. No, that wasn't it. It was as if he knew if he took his hand, something would happen to him he wouldn't like. Dan looked for handcuffs. He'd seen that on his shows where the man would cuff—he had to focus.

"I've come for my wife. Kala Carey. Could you please ask her to come out so we can be on our way? I need to get this car back to our neighbor before they get too upset with me. I had thought that it wouldn't take this long to get here." Again, the thought that it shouldn't have nudged at his mind, but it was gone before he could hold onto it.

Dan tried not to think about the numerous car calls he'd gotten while he'd been coming here. The calls had startled him at first. And when the steering wheel had spoken to him to ask him if he would take the call, he'd said yes before he could remember that the car did not belong to him.

His neighbor was the caller, and he screamed at Dan for several minutes before Dan was able to find the end button. But it did little good. The man called and called until Dan wanted to scream at him. In the end, he told the man that he'd given him the car to use and it was unfair of him to take it back now. He told Dan that he hadn't let Dan borrow it, and then he started shouting again. Finally, Dan had had to make sure the calls didn't come in again and stabbed a knife in the steering wheel. Kala would have to make sure she paid that first.

"She's not your wife." The words, spoken softly, startled him, and Dan looked at the man again. "Kala isn't your wife. Surely you remember that. She was your co-worker. At the cable company." It took Dan several seconds to remember what he was there for, and then smiled at the man.

"Yes, that's where we met. She and I were let go on the same day." Dan smiled again at the man, wondering why he'd say such a thing, and Dan tried to reassure him that Kala was indeed his wife. "She and I were married three weeks ago. She said yes and we couldn't wait, so we went to the justice of the peace and he married us."

"No, that's not true." The man sat down on the step as he continued. "And three weeks ago you were running from the law. You killed your mother about then. Then the other two people shortly after. And then there was Randy and his wife, Connie. You've been very busy since you got canned from the cable company. But, like I said, Kala is not your wife."

Dan didn't like what this man was saying. He felt his head start to hurt, and he took a step back from him. When Kala came out of the house, he nearly went to her, but the man stood up beside her. Things were not right, and Dan wasn't sure how to make them right. His nose started to fill, and he knew he was going to get a nosebleed. He'd not had one of those since he was younger.

"Dan Carey, this is my wife, Kala." Dan felt his head explode in pain. As he dropped to his knees, a white hot rage poured over him, and Dan had to hold his hands together so he wouldn't hurt anyone.

"Momma said not to hurt people. Not to hurt people, not to hurt people, not to hurt people." Dan looked up when someone touched his head and saw it was his Kala. "I won't hurt you."

"I know that. You're very sick, aren't you?" Dan shook his head. "Come on. Stand up. You're going to tell me what you've been doing with yourself. And then we're going to get you some help. All right?"

"You have to come home with me, Kala. It's all I can think about right now. The house is a mess, and I think my room needs to be finished. But you can do that, can't you? You can fix everything just by coming with me. Tell me that's what you're going to do." Kala helped him stand up, and he tried to pull her toward the car. "Come on with me, Kala. I have to take the car back. The neighbor said I could only have it for an hour." When she pulled free of him, he felt the blood pour from his nose. Wiping at it, he knew that this was more than before. There was so much blood on his hand that he could only stare at it.

"Dan, look at me." He looked at her face and could see that she'd changed somehow. He wasn't sure how, but he knew she had. "You didn't borrow this car. You stole it. Don't lie to me again." Her voice was firm, like his momma's used to be when she was upset with him about something. Dan started to shake his head, but it hurt too much.

"I didn't." She was backing away from him as he continued. "That's right, Kala. I promise you. He said I could borrow it. I asked him. I did. He even gave me the keys. See? I have them in the car. Just come with me and everything will be all right. You'll see."

"You stole the car, and if you don't tell me the truth, I'm finished talking to you." He tried to think, but she kept talking. "You hit him with his car when he came out to stop you. He has a broken leg, and his arm is messed up so that he's going to miss work. If he loses his job over this, it will be sad for him. You did this, Dan. You've been very bad, and now there are a lot of people dead and so many hurt lives because of you. You need help."

"I ran over the trash can. Not a person. Don't you think I'd know if I ran over a person with a car?" Kala shook her head when he tried to laugh it off. "The police were there. They can tell you. I was leaving, and the trashcan was there."

"It was Mr. Bishop. You ran over him when he tried to stop you. The police were there because you killed an officer when she came to bring you in. She had three children and a husband. Do you remember that? What about the other people you killed? Your own mother? Do you remember slicing open her throat and putting her in the basement?" Dan shook his head. The pain was making him sick. "And Randy and his wife Connie. She was beaten to death with a ball bat, and you took Randy's head —"

"No. That's not right. The police did it to frame me. They don't want us together. No one does." Kala moved away from him and toward the man on the porch. When Dan reached for her, it was only to be brought up short by the man grabbing his hand. "I have to take my wife home. You have to let me go. This is not right. I need my wife."

Dan could feel the tears flowing now. He couldn't help it. He was hurting, and he was sick. Kala wasn't being herself right now, and he had a sudden thought that she might need medications too. But Dan looked at her and saw that while he was a mess, and he knew that he was, she looked as pretty as she always did.

Even more so, he thought. When she spoke again, Dan held his head. It was too much.

"I'm not going anywhere with you, Dan. You've been lying to everyone, and it has to stop. I'm not your wife, I'm Riss's wife. I love him, not you."

Dan tried to think what to do now. She wasn't going to come with him. He needed her to make the pain stop. She was the only one who could do it. Smiling at her while he still held his head, Dan thought to reason with her. It worked before when he wanted something from her.

"Kala, we got off on the wrong thing here. I guess you might be right that we're not married. But the other stuff, that's just not right. I had nothing to do with that. You know me better than that. I'm a good person, you told me that enough. You wanted me to get a place of my own, and now that Momma's gone we can have that. I just need you to come with me so you can help me." His nose was running, and he wiped at it several times, smearing the blood on the front of his shirt. There was so much blood that he was worried. Looking up at Kala, he showed her what was going on. "Look at this."

Dizzy, Dan dropped to his knees. Weakness, something his momma always called him, was making him not able to stand any longer. There was no stopping him from falling forward. And he was thankful for it. Maybe he'd feel better laying down. He saw the dirt coming toward him at a quick pace, but he couldn't move his hands up to stop it. As soon as his face hit the drive, he felt as if he had been run over. He looked up when someone rolled him over to his back. His Kala was finally coming to him.

"Look at me." Kala was shouting at him, but he couldn't do anything about it. She told him three more times to keep his eyes open, but it was just too hard. He couldn't even reach out to her to touch her face. Every part of him felt as if he were covered in lead. Dan knew he was going to die.

"My head hurts." He knew what he wanted to say but it sounded odd when he heard it. "Kala?"

"Breathe, Dan. Just breathe." The man standing over him and talking now was different than the other one. This man looked like he could break him in half. "You're having a stroke. You have to breathe, Dan. Don't close your eyes either. I need you to stay with me."

"I can't. I have to protect Kala. Murderer out there." Dan didn't know if the man understood him or not because Dan closed his eyes again. He was floating now and felt his body begin to feel strange. There was another man, but this man didn't look mad or upset like the other two. This one looked very sad.

"You're not ready to come here yet. I just wanted to let you know that you're going to get the best of care." Dan felt weightless and his head no longer hurt. But the man touched him on the forehead and he felt as if he was coming up out of the water.

Dan still couldn't move, but he felt better. His head didn't hurt, and the room he was in looked very nice. Clean and all white like this, he thought he could live here forever. When he tried to look around, all he could see was white, and Dan frowned. There wasn't a single television in this place. Then a man with wings was there. Dan vaguely remembered him from a long time ago.

"Hello, Daniel. My name is Robert. I'm going to protect you from now on." Dan started to ask him about his shows, but he seemed to know. "Soon. When you're out of recovery, I'll bring you a television."

Something had happened to him, and Dan wasn't sure what it had been. His mind was clear now, of everything, and he knew that he'd done some pretty bad things. Dan tried to open his eyes to see if someone could tell him what was going on, but it hurt too much. Instead of fighting it, he let go and looked at Robert. For whatever reason, it felt good to see him standing there, and Dan knew that no one would be able to frame him for anything ever again.

~~~

Kala paced the waiting room as they waited on word from the surgeon. He told them that he'd be back as soon as he could, but that had been hours ago. Kala thought for sure Dan had died and no one had told her yet. She knew that he'd done some really horrible things, but she still didn't want him to die. Not like this.

"He's not dead." Kala looked over at Agon, who had been at the hospital when they'd arrived. He told her he was a protector, like Riss had been. He'd also told her that he was with Dan the entire time and had brought him to her.

"How do you know? And why aren't you with him now?" She flushed when he winked at her. "What are you doing here?"

"I'm Riss's friend. Yours, too, if you can learn to tone down the attitude." Kala opened her mouth and closed it when he stood. She wasn't sure what she was going to say to him, but his size scared her a little. When he came closer to her, she took a step back. The man had to be seven feet tall.

"I'm six foot, ten inches. And I would never harm you." Kala nodded at him. "You don't believe me? That's okay. You don't know me, and that's reason enough for you not to trust me. But believe me when I say, for you I would die. In answer to your question, I'm not Daniel's protector. His is Robert. I'm...let's just call it stronger than Robert is, and I was able to get through to Daniel when no one else could. You could say that it's my specialty."

"Does everyone have a specialty? Never mind. I don't think I want to know that right now. And as for dying for me, that won't be necessary." He shrugged at her. "I'm sorry. You must think I'm a real bitch. I know it's no excuse, but I'm really scared for Dan. He might be...he is everything they say he is, but he was my friend first. The only one I had for a long time."

"And for that reason alone, you are mine as well." She didn't understand him, and he seemed to know it and explained, "You have a big heart and see the goodness in others that we might miss. We, all of us older protectors, are jaded somewhat. When Riss had said he was quitting the job, leaving us, I was...I thought if he can do this, then I can, too. I've been thinking that it might be the thing I need to do as well. Quit, not find a wife. I've no use for one at my age."

"You wish to die?" He nodded. "I'm so sorry to hear that. I don't know what you do for Boss, but I'd...." She smiled at him, and he raised a brow. Kala had a feeling that he wanted her to be afraid of him more than friendly with him. "Why don't you come and work with Riss and me? We were told we could pick our own team."

He threw back his head and laughed. Then he hugged her to him, and she felt a strange connection run up her arms where they touched. When he pulled back, he looked at her oddly before kissing her on the forehead. She found it a little weird that he'd nearly had to bend in half to do so.

"You are with child." Kala put her hand on her belly and nodded at him. "Good. And I would be honored to come and work with you and Riss. But...." They both looked down the hallway when the surgeon came toward them. When someone took her hand, she didn't even bother looking but gripped it tightly as he walked toward her. The connection was so tight between this man and her that she knew that if this was bad news, he'd be there for her.

"Let's have a seat, why don't we?" When they were settled, Kala looked around at all the other people with her. They were her support team. Kala looked at the doctor.

"I'm a person who likes it said and not going around the bush seven times before I get it. Say what's going on and I can deal with it." He grinned and nodded.

"There was...Mr. Carey did have a stroke, but it wasn't as bad as we'd first thought. When we took him into surgery, we were concerned by the blood loss and did some x-rays of his brain. There we found a tumor. A very large one that has been pressing against his brain for what I would guess the last twenty years." Kala nodded and felt Riss sit beside her as the doctor continued. "We have removed as much of it as we can, but I'm afraid that the damage is still there. Had it been caught years ago, he might have lived a long and productive life. As it is...I don't believe Mr. Carey will ever leave a long term facility."

"How did it get missed for so long?" She watched his face and saw the anger there and knew. "No one cared enough to look for it. They thought there was something wrong with him mentally and never bothered to look to see what else was going on."

"That would be my guess. They knew that he'd had issues as a child, and instead of treating what might have been wrong with him, they gave him drugs to keep him down. And when that failed to work, they gave him more and more. While Mr. Carey did kill all those people, I would guess that a large part of that blame is on the medical field as well as his mother. From the records I've seen, he was abused as a child, and it never got any better as he grew older. I would say that the only reason it might have stopped when he reached adulthood was either because she herself had been incapacitated or he was too big for her to control. He was an abused person, no two ways about it."

When he left them a few minutes later, Kala sat alone on the couch. The rest of them were talking in low tones, but she didn't want to join them. She had a lot to think about, and very little of it had to do with the people that were there. Looking up when she felt a presence, she glared at Boss for several seconds until she asked Him to leave her alone.

"Daniel will die at peace." She looked at Him as He sat down. "I'm sorry for your loss, Kala. Daniel might have been a good man had someone tried to help him as you've done, but it was much too late when he met you. He would not have had that had you not been with him in his final moments before this. I'm so very sorry."

"And that's supposed to make me feel better?" He didn't answer her but watched her. "He had a brain tumor. Couldn't one of his watchers have told someone about it? Or made someone look into it? Why would this happen to someone like him? It wasn't his fault."

"No, most of it wasn't his fault, but he did them all the same. Things had to progress the way they did with as little involvement as possible from us." She snorted at Him. "I'm sorry that you don't feel we did a good job with this, but—"

"Save it. You let all those people be killed because you couldn't interfere. If you couldn't do that, who the hell could?" Boss leaned back on the couch, and she got up to pace. She was mad, and He might as well take the brunt of her anger.

"You would have me take care of everyone in the entire world? Drop everything when someone bumps their knee?" She started to tell Him this was much more than a bumped knee when He continued. "Where would you have me draw the line, Kala? With broken bones? Cancer victims? Who do you suppose should get all of the attention we can give them, and who will be left out when there are not enough men and women to go around? You think I don't die a little each and every time something like this happens? You think that I don't know that we should do more but cannot? I care more than you can imagine."

"He was my friend." Kala looked at Him when He didn't comment. "I've said this before, but I do believe he was my only friend for a long time. He was there for me when I needed him to be. I had no idea about the other stuff, his infatuation with me, but regardless of that, he was there when I needed him to be." Boss nodded and put out His hands, motioning to the people down the hall.

"All of them are our friends as well. Most of them have only just met you and still they consider themselves lucky to have you here for them. For Riss. What would you say if I told you that three of the people standing there will be dead in the next ten years? And that two more of them will have their bodies broken so badly that they will be in pain for the rest of their days? Days that they will think very seriously about ending their lives." Kala looked down the hall to the people standing there.

She knew that five of them were protectors, including Riss. Seven were humans and three that she didn't know what they were. When she turned back to Him, Boss was wiping at a tear, and her heart went out to Him.

"Daily I deal with death, Kala. Not in a small scale, but seconds do not go by that I don't feel the pain of someone's passing. That even the smallest of creatures pass tears at each of us who watch over them." Boss stood up and turned her to face Him, and she could see His pain. "I will tell you something else, Kala. The child you now carry? The first of our kind to be born and not made? He will have his fair share of pain and hurt, but he will be stronger for it. Just as the people who love him."

"I'm sorry." He nodded but let her go. "Please forgive me. I'm...I know this isn't much, but I'm sorry to have taken this out on you. I don't know why, but you seemed to be...I feel like I can talk to you like I can no one else. I should have taken better care with my words. It was wrong of me to take my hurt out on you when I can see you hurt just as much as I do."

"We are going to be good friends, my dear Kala. This I swear to you. Daniel's passing will be a fading, nothing like his life had been. It will be quiet and without fan fair. No one will grieve his passing but you, and none will care that he killed, not for the sake of murder, but because he was never loved."

"That's the saddest thing I've ever heard." He told her it was. "I'm sorry. Truly, I am. I never meant to insult you or anyone else."

"You are a good woman, Kala. Strong and willful. Enough to keep Riss on his toes and me thinking of visiting you more often than I should. I believe you will be a good addition to our teams." Kala nodded. "Have you thought of a last name as yet? You and Riss, I mean?"

"I think so. We are going to be Riss and Kala Trainer." Boss nodded. "It was Riss's idea. He thought it was something people would remember better. The Trainers."

"No one will forget you once they have met you. This is a trueness that I will give you to hold in your heart. As for your name, I love it. It suits." He nodded and moved to go to the others, but stopped. "Kala, do not ever change, please. I think you are perfect in every way you are."

She wasn't really sure what that meant but nodded anyway. When He was gone down the hall, she sat down again. When Riss came toward her, she smiled at him. He looked so good to her that she wanted to keep him in her pocket.

"You do know that we can talk to each other all the time, even when we're not together." She nodded. "Did you and Boss have a nice talk?"

"He thinks our last name is perfect." Riss picked her up and put her on his lap as she continued. "Do you suppose we'll have any problems registering our names? I mean, we weren't married in a traditional sort of way."

"We have helpers throughout the government. Most of them are humans, but there are a few that aren't. We have found a need for them, and they can do just about anything. I believe that we've been filed in the local offices as married. And I contacted someone this morning to have our last name changed as well." She snuggled onto his shoulder.

"Lily and I are having lunch tomorrow. She's coming by the house. I didn't know that protectors had to be held in a safe place. Doesn't the whole immortal thing kinda keep them safe anyway?"

Riss smacked her ass before he answered her. "You're an immortal, too. Please remember that. And she doesn't mean she feels safe there. It's more of a being free thing. Her wings can be freed, and she doesn't have to worry about anyone turning her in for being a freak. Also, there's the added bonus of being with you. That in and of itself is a real plus."

Kala didn't know about all of that, but she didn't say anything. She liked Lily and enjoyed talking to her. Kala had been making a list of questions to sit down and talk to her about anyway. And this was the best way. As they gathered up to leave, she asked if she could see Dan just one time. Riss helped her find someone who could help her with that.

"You'll need to not touch him. His body is very sensitive right now." Kala nodded to the nurse, who was showing her to the room where he was. Kala noticed the police everywhere and wondered if he'd be watched like this for the rest of his life. Probably. He had killed a great many people.

Kala was shocked by what Dan looked like. Most of his head and face were covered in bandages, and there were bloodstains all over them. She knew from the doctor that they'd had to take a great portion of his skull off and hadn't been able to replace it until the swelling went down. There were also tubes and wires all over him. Kala sat down in the only chair and looked at the man who had come to mean a great deal to her, but not necessarily in a good way.

"I don't know what to say to you. You should have told me sooner what you felt. I don't know what I would have done, but this was off the chart in stupidity." Her anger at him dissipated once she started talking. "I was always there for you, Dan. All you had to do was talk to me. Tell me how you felt. There was never any reason for this to get this far."

She could see him hanging his head in shame, something that he always did when she corrected something he'd said or done. He'd been like a big puppy to her, and she had to smile. Trying her best not to cry again at the sadness of it all, she tried to be a little more upbeat.

"I'm happy now. Happier than I ever thought possible. Riss and his friends have taken me in and have treated me so well. I think maybe...." She looked away, trying to fight the tears again, and lost the battle. "You were such a good friend to me when I needed one. I hate that this happened to you. I'm so sorry. But I understand that you were sick and needed more than anyone would give you. For that I wish I could do something more for you."

Kala thought about the people that lost their lives because of him. The Shields and Officer McKay. Both of them had families that would miss them. McKay, she'd heard, had three children and a husband. There were others, too, who had died because of the man lying before her. And Dan's mother had also died.

"I've heard some things about your mother from Mr. Bishop. He said that she wasn't a nice person. He told me that as you got bigger he thought things were different because they didn't see you beaten up like you'd been, but there were still shouts coming from the house. Mr. Bishop said he called the police only because you'd taken your mother's car. I guess he'd called several times to Family Services on her about her treatment of you. I had no idea that she'd tied you to a tree for days on end when you were bad." Mr. Bishop had told her a great deal more, but Kala didn't want to think of that now. Some of the things that Dan had had to endure were too much for her to think about. "I'm making arrangements for you to be put into a facility that will give you good care. I...Riss and I are going to visit you, too. Every week. I'm going to get me a reader to take, and I'm going to read to you. Mr. Bishop told me that you loved to read."

The nurse came in and told her that her time was up. Kala looked at Dan and wanted to take his hand into hers. At the last minute she did, touched him with just her fingers, and felt a connection. She looked up to see Robert, Dan's protector.

"I will watch over him for you. Our connection is there again, just different." Kala nodded her thanks and started for the door when Robert spoke again. "He knows that you're here, my lady. He is saddened by what he's done and asks that you forgive him."

"He has nothing for me to forgive him for. What he needs to do is ask it of someone higher than me." Robert smiled and nodded. "You'll tell him?"

"I have. Thank you." Kala left the little room and walked to Riss. There, she stood with his arms wrapped around her and felt safer than she'd ever been in her life.

"Let's go home." And she knew that within seconds of her saying it, they were just where they wanted to be. At home. Their home.

Chapter 13

"I have a list that I started. I'm not sure that over the weeks ahead that I won't add to it, but this is the start." Lily tried her best not to laugh. She really liked Kala and was glad for her humor. But Lily had a feeling that she wasn't joking and nodded for her to begin. "Okay. This isn't really a biggy, but I do want to know. Why am I the first to have a child? I mean, you're here, and I'm assuming you're not the only female. So what gives?"

"There are a great many of us here apparently. I had to ask when you'd mentioned it the other day. But as to your question, you were human when you conceived, as was Riss when he came to you. Had you become his wife before you had sex, then you, too, would be childless. It's not something we do, have sex with humans." Lily knew that she could expound on that but wanted to see her mind work. Boss said it was an amazing thing to see.

"Human. I guess you mean that when he came to me, for all intents and purposes he could have died." Lily shook her head, wondering where this was going. "You mean he was still a protector?"

"No. He was a human but an immortal one. All his…parts worked then. As a protector, he is built just like man, only he does not function like one. Such as, his reproductive organs will not produce a child, but he can still function like a man." Lily felt her face heat up. "This is a strange conversation, even for me.

Kala nodded before speaking. "You mean he could have fucked me, just not impregnated me if he was the protector but not human. Okay, I get it I guess. He would have been able to father a child to any human while he was pretending to be a human."

"No, only you." Kala got up to go to the refrigerator, and Lily watched her. She was a sight to behold when she was working through something. When the glass of tea was set in front of her, Lily watched her put a tin of cookies down too before she said what was on her mind. Lily took two of the chocolate chip cookies, and was biting into one when Kala spoke.

"Did he have sex before me?" Lily wanted to laugh but was choking on the crumbs that got stuck in her throat when Kala finally opened her mouth. As she pounded her on the back, Kala continued. "I mean, you guys can pretty much see the people you protect naked and doing things I'm pretty sure if I thought about would embarrass me a great deal."

"No, he hadn't had sex before. It is not in our nature to do that. It's actually forbidden. We are...we don't...." Lily smiled. "We don't have a desire for our charges because most of us have seen them from birth to death. They are like our children."

"But you did Benny." Lily shook her head. "You didn't feel desire for Benny when you first met him?"

"He was not my charge when he was a baby. I came to him when he was a teenager. His charge was moved around. I believe now it was planned from the beginning." It wasn't until Lily met Kala and got to know the story behind her and Riss that she'd figured that one out. "I knew who he was to me from the start of my keeping him safe. I accidently showed myself to him when he turned twenty-five. He'd been harmed in a gun exchange, and I'd...I had to bring him back to me. I found that living without him after that was impossible. Boss granted me permission to stay with him. We were married a few months later."

Kala looked at her list for a long time before she looked up at her. "This will be the only child we have."

Lily felt her pain. She could understand it. She herself had felt the same when she realized how much she wanted to have a child by Benny. But there was so much more that Kala could do, something that she and Benny had talked about.

"It will be the only child you carry, but not the only one you can have. There are things you are not aware of as yet. Then there are hundreds of human children out there that will need love and understanding. Someone to care for them as a protector would. I believe that we can offer a child like that more than they can get living in a foster home."

"I lived in one for most of my life." Lily had forgotten about that and started to apologize to her. "No, please don't. I had it better than most. I was never adopted, but I didn't suffer overly much for it. When I was eighteen, I left and have been...I guess 'happy' could be the word to use. I wasn't harmed, no one tried to molest me, but I was an oddity to most of the other children. Being a red head can do that for you."

"I love your hair. It suits you so much." Lily flushed when Kala laughed. "I meant no harm to you."

"No, I was just thinking about what Boss said before He left me yesterday. He told me not to change, He liked me this way. I think He meant my bad temper and smart mouth. What do you think?" Lily laughed, too.

"I would say that He likes you for both, but He finds it refreshing for someone to challenge Him on occasion. I think you do that." Lily nodded to the list. "What else do you have for me?"

They worked through her list for the rest of the day. Most of her questions were brilliant, and some of them Lily had no answer for. When she left, she was going to see if Boss could help her with them and hoped that she and Kala could get together more often. Lily especially liked that Kala wanted to see if it were possible to set up a place where they could help out the less fortunate by helping them get jobs.

"When I went to my first job interview, I had no idea what to expect. And my clothes were out of date and worn. We could find a way to get donations to supply them with something nice to wear."

Lily found herself getting excited too. "I know of a few professors that could help with their resumes as well. Maybe we can get a few business owners to give mock interviews. That would help, I believe." Lily wanted to do this. She worked a great deal because Benny did, but they'd talked about taking more time for each other. Lily was going to get him to help her with this as soon as she got home. Then she'd raid both their closets. She knew for a fact there were things in there that were older than the young woman in front of her.

Kala had started a list. It had things they were both going to do on it and who they were to contact to do it. Lily hadn't had this much fun in decades, and felt good about giving something back to the world. When she was handed her list of things to do just before she left, she hugged the younger woman and felt wonderful when she returned the hug.

"There is something you should know about your child." Kala started to shake her head, and Lily nodded. "It is important. I swear to you that you'll need this information sooner rather than later."

"There's nothing wrong with him, is there?" Lily put her hand over Kala's belly and smiled at her.

"There is nothing wrong with any of them." Lily waited for her to understand what she was saying. When Kala finally did, Lily burst out laughing from the expression on her face.

"Them? As in more than one?" Lily nodded and helped Kala sit down. "I think I'm going to be sick."

"No you won't, and you should know that you are going to be a wonderful mother. And have so many babysitters lined up that you'll never have to worry about."

Kala nodded, then looked up and asked how many.

"You will have four. Would you like to know the sex?"

"No. I...no, I don't think so." Lily nodded and waited. "You aren't kidding me, are you? I'm really going to have quadruplets? Four little protectors all at once? How the hell am I supposed to help train others if I'm forever exhausted from watching these guys?"

"You will do wonderfully, and you will not be tired doing so. And I would never kid about a thing such as this. Isn't it wonderful? Instead of just a single child, they will have siblings. They will be happier for it too." Lily sat down across from her new friend and smiled. "You and I are the only ones that know. Riss can tell the sex but not the count. Boss knows, I'm sure, and is right now laughing at you, but He will not tell either."

"Four... four children. I have no idea what I'm doing." Lily laughed at her. "What if I mess them up? What if they hate me?"

"You are their mother and they will love you more than anything else. And there is no way you can mess them up. First of all, you're much too smart for that, and secondly...well there is no reason for a second reason. You simply will not."

Lily left her an hour later, armed with her list and a mission to get it finished before they met again. Knowing that the woman was going to have four children made her want to talk to Benny now, but she waited and made her own list. The sooner they got their names on the list for adoption the better. Lily was excited about the prospect of having someone call her mom as well. And Benny would be glad for a son as well. Lily thought they'd make wonderful parents.

~~~

Riss came into the house just before dawn. He'd been working with some of the other protectors and had lost track of time. He'd talked to Kala twice, and the last time he'd reached for her he realized she had gone to bed. Standing over her now, sleeping so peacefully, he wanted to wake her to tell her how much he loved her, but moved to the other side and stripped down to join her.

Her body was warm, and he hated to pull her to his cold one, but as soon as he lay down, she turned and snuggled to him. When she was wrapped around him, he felt the weight of the world slide off him. Riss held her as tightly as he could as he closed his eyes. At peace, Riss thought he could take on the world.

"Do you want something to eat?" Her voice startled him slightly, as he hadn't realized she was awake. Lifting his head to look down at her, she smiled up at him as she continued. "I can fix you something if you want. I'm not a very good cook, but I can open a can of soup with the best of them."

"I have all I need right here." Riss felt her smile against his throat as he pulled her close again. "What have you been doing today? Did Lily answer all your questions?"

He'd been sort of hurt at first that she'd not asked him. Then when she'd told him how excited she was to have a woman-friend coming over, he realized it was more than just a question and answer thing but more of a girl thing. It was impossible for him to think that she'd had so few friends. Everyone that had met her over the past few weeks had fallen in love with her. Riss had left her that morning happy because she was meeting Lily. And he realized as he'd been working on the new training center that that was all life was about, being happy.

"We did. And she and I are going to start a job service. To help people get a job." He could hear the excitement in her voice and felt it wash over him. "I told her about how I'd had so much trouble getting my first job because I had no clue what I was supposed to say or even wear. Lily said she is going to see about using one of the buildings downtown to rent. There are so many of them for sale, we thought maybe we could get them for a good deal to use for this. We're going to get help from some of her other teacher friends and set up some interviews and things. For practice. We have some things we can start on now, but mostly it's going to be begging for help. And, of course, for money."

"I have some. Money I mean. I'm not sure what it amounts to, but there is a great deal of it, I believe. I never spent any of it when I was a protector, and we would get paid in script or however we wanted. When

185

I expressed a desire to have a house, all of it was converted to the currency from this realm." Sitting up, he reached for the notebook he'd started carrying around with him when he'd become earthbound. Mostly it held questions he had. He found that he enjoyed looking them up, but he'd also gotten into the habit of writing down how much he spent from the cash he had. There was a balance of his accounts in the back. "I was told that my payment from my job as a protector could be moved to a human account. I don't know what it is worth, but the man who helped me to set it up said that we'd be able to live comfortably for a very long time. And Boss said He'd continue to pay me, as well as you, for our help."

He found the page and handed the notebook to her. She looked at it for several seconds, then at him. Riss was worried it wasn't enough to support them when she kissed him on the mouth.

"You have no idea how much money you have, do you?" He shook his head. Money had never been an issue with him, and now was not really much different. "Riss, you have over ten billion dollars here. You could buy a small country with that much money."

"Why would we want to do that?" She laughed, and he frowned. "I don't understand you sometimes. Is that a good thing? Enough to buy a small country? I would just like for us to be happy. And if we need something, we can go and purchase it."

She kissed him again, and he found that he was enjoying this much more than he should. When she pulled away this time, he pulled her back to deepen the kiss. Before he could find out the answer to his next question, he forgot what it was. Rolling her to her back after pulling her toward him completely, he looked down at her.

"You are the most precious thing in the world to me." Riss leaned down and nibbled at her nipple through her shirt. "And I think I fall in love with you more daily."

"I love you as well." He kissed her again and removed her shirt when she moaned. "Riss, love, if you don't take me now, I'm going to hurt you."

"Always in such a hurry. I would enjoy exploring the parts of you that I missed before." He slid his hand up her arm, stretching it out so that it was above her head. When he thought about the scarf he'd purchased for her just to tie her up, he wrapped it around her wrist and tied it to the headboard. He did the same to the other arm.

"You may keep your legs untied until you no longer behave. Understand?" Her nod was the most erotic thing he'd ever seen. The fact that she was willing to let him have his way was making him ache to have her come. "I will allow you to come, but you must do so without making a sound."

"I won't be able to do that. You make me scream just when you touch me." Riss nipped at her throat as she continued. "See, you're killing me already and you've only just started."

"You'll be all right, love. I promise you that you'll enjoy this more than you can imagine." Her snort of disbelief made him smile. "Shall I show you?"

He took her breast into his mouth and suckled hard. He could feel her body rock up to meet his, and he wondered if his plan was backfiring. When suddenly she whimpered, he looked up.

"I want to come." Riss nodded. "No, you don't understand. I need to scream out my release. It's not the same when I can't."

"I don't understand." He shifted over her and felt his cock at her entrance. Heat seemed to suck him in even through her clothing, and he moaned. "You're going to make me hurry, aren't you?"

"No. Please, Riss, I need you. Don't stop. I'll try to behave." He knew that she would, too, so he decided to double his efforts to make her scream. The first thing he did was tie her legs to the bed.

"You are going to enjoy this." He moved his hands down her body, removing the rest of her clothing but her panties and bra. "Your skin is like the silk you wear. So soft and smooth. I love the way it heats under my hand, the way you flush when I touch you."

Her nipples were so hard now he could see them pressing against her bra. Riss nuzzled his face between the large orbs and inhaled deeply. She smelled of heaven. Moving to her shoulders, he kissed his way to her elbow and then the crook of her arm. There he licked his way up to her wrist where he bit down on her pounding pulse.

Kala was writhing now. Her body undulating up and down, and he wanted to enter her and take her now, but this was proving to be much more fun than he'd thought possible. As he took each of her fingers into his mouth and suckled them, he watched her face. It was lovely, and he leaned over to kiss her.

"You're driving me crazy," she told him breathlessly. "Just so you know, when it's my turn, I'm showing you no mercy."

"Agreed." He felt his cock jerk as he thought of being tied to her bed and lifted her bra up to take the morsel into his mouth. Her body responded by rolling upward, and Riss ran his hand down her body to her femininity. "Come for me, Kala. I want to see the look on your face when you do."

She cried out, and under the circumstances, he didn't care if she brought the house down on them. Watching her get her relief was most wonderful sight he'd ever seen. When he commanded her to come again, she did so, screaming out his name as he slid his fingers into her. He had to taste her, take in her creaminess when she came again.

Moving down her body, Riss took small nibbles of her everywhere he could. Her body was dewy with her climaxes, and he found he loved even the taste of that. When he was at the juncture of her thighs, Riss removed her panties, the last barrier to what he wanted. He spread her wider still and suckled her into his mouth. Her juices filled his mouth and he had to swallow fast to get it all. When she came again, he lapped at her over and over until she begged him to stop. Still it wasn't enough. There was so much of her to explore this way that he wanted to take notes so as not to miss an inch of her ever.

"Please, Riss, no more. I can't take any more." Riss knew that she could and told her so. "If I come again, I'm going to pass out. I swear to you, I can't take—"

He entered her hard, slamming himself to his balls inside of her. Letting her go, taking away all the silken wrappings around her limbs, he felt her wrap around him even as he pounded. Riss felt his balls filled and tightened to his body in an almost painful way. And when he came, his body bowing back from hers, he felt his eyes roll to the back of his head as every nerve ending in his body felt electrified. But still he moved in and out of her, deeper, harder until he was spent from it. Dropping down atop her, Riss felt his body go limp and wondered if he'd be able to move if anything came to harm them. Closing his eyes, he let exhaustion take him.

The next time he woke, he knew that something wasn't right. Sitting up slowly so as not to wake Kala, he reached for his pants just as someone touched his mind. He moved to the door as the person spoke. Riss didn't find Boss there any more comforting than he did anyone at the moment. But he knew that someone had been watching them. Riss wondered if they had a protector and wanted to talk to Boss about it.

"For the time being, I think it should be that way. There is no one in your bedroom, nor can they hear you when you are...enjoying yourselves. But I think for now at least, someone should be close at all times. I was thinking that we must talk. Is now a good time?" Riss grabbed a shirt and told Him he could meet Him in the dining room. *"That would be splendid. I have taken the liberty of bringing you in a cook. I hope you do not mind. But waiting for you proved to be longer than I had expected, and I grew hungry for some human cuisine."*

"We were working on that, but we've been sort of busy." Riss made his way to the dining room to find Boss and two people that he'd never seen. "You've hired a staff as well?"

"No. They came to meet with Kala. She and I have talked, and I think it best that she choose who helps her with the household, don't you? She is going to be...I think she will need the extra hands when the delivery comes." It took Riss a few seconds to realize He meant the birth of his son. "She is well, I take it? No lingering afterthoughts about what happened with her friend?"

"She is upset, but I think it's more because she doesn't understand yet what all happened. She does blame his mother a great deal. Mr. Bishop, the neighbor, has talked with her as well. I don't think that Daniel had a very good life. I think she's very happy too. She and Lily had a good time today. I think we might be in for some hard work ahead with their plans. But they'll make it work." Boss nodded and smiled at him. Riss flushed, thinking how happy he'd made her and changed the subject. "I wanted to find out how this thing with the training is going to work. I know what my job was but am not sure how to train others to do it. When I was created to watch over humans, the knowledge was there already."

"As it will be with them. But they will lack the...I guess I would call it the finer tuning that you have now. The things that you learned over the years. Years and years of experience, as it were. You can teach them how to keep from being too bored as well." Boss handed him a thick book, and when Riss put his hand on it, he felt all the knowledge within enter his mind and his heart. "This information will guide you and Kala. She will need it most, I think. The rules haven't changed all that much, but there are things, with this training, that I'd very much like to work through before we introduce it to the new protectors."

"You mean the new way that we're to bring them over? Or are you talking about the system that you mention about the little ones. That is the hardest part, I think. Even more so than watching animals. Bringing a child to our arms...it's the hardest thing I've ever done." Riss knew what the plans were for the other men such as him. "I think that you should know that there are others like me, ones that might come to you in the near future to leave. I'm sorry, but you must know that, like you, we are weary of it all. You believe that...what I mean is, do you...?"

Riss was at a loss. The other men that he'd worked with, they had felt the same as he had over the last decades, wanting to quit their services enough to die for it. Riss hadn't known of the others, the men and women that now populated the earth that were once protectors. He'd known of Lily, but never knew that she had been put here with her husband. Riss had always thought that she'd simply been a person to help with a service they might need.

"I know that I would rather this path be taken than the one you had planned." Riss looked away, feeling foolish for his thoughts on dying. He would have missed so much. "Riss? You were right in thinking it was the only way. I gave you no other option. Now I am extending this to the others, but they must not know. Not yet at least. I know of one or two of your brethren that will not come easily if they think this is my plan."

"I understand. They would...I'm sure there would be arguments from a few." Galin for one, Riss thought, and Valyn if what he'd talked about while they'd been working was any indication. He did not like humans in a personal sense at all, and would fight this to the very end. "Tholan as well? He doesn't...I thought he enjoyed his job, but I've come to the conclusion that he is just as ready as I'd been. Maybe a bit more so."

"I believe you to be correct. Tholan has been...I'm sure you understand when I say that what I have planned is mine alone. Michael knows of some but not all. And you will know what I deem necessary for you to know. But for now, it is time that I have a good meal and leave. The hours grow ever shorter." Riss knew that whatever other questions he had would not be answered. Boss had spoken, and it was as good as done.

They enjoyed a fine dinner of fried chicken and mashed potatoes. There was an apple pie for dessert, and Riss found it hard not to have a second piece. But he did have the cooks save a plate for Kala. He wondered what she would think of dining with Boss once a week as he'd asked to do.

When Boss stood, so did Riss.

"You'll come back weekly then? We'd like that. I think that Kala enjoys your company." Boss snorted, and Riss had to laugh. "Okay, she likes to argue with you. But I think you enjoy it as much as she does."

"I do. She is a good woman and will help you in ways you will not believe." Riss knew that already. He was in love with his wife and would be for the rest of his days. Boss cleared His throat, and Riss looked up at Him. "You'll be starting in a week, I think. The compound will be ready, and I'll have a list of names for you to begin with. We will start slowly, as I've said, to work out what we really need for you to train with and what can be learned only in the field. As for your first trainees, Argon and Valyn will be around to help you get them into shape. I think it best for all if that is the case. Valyn will train Kala with her wings, as will Lily. The two of them have taken to each other better than I thought they would."

Riss nodded and made a mental note to talk to Kala. She would love having Lily around, but Valyn could be...well, he was somewhat of a serious protector and wouldn't know how to handle her humor or temper. Then again, Kala might rub off on him, and he'd maybe smile once in a while.

"Valyn will be fine, Riss. I would not have paired him with Kala if I didn't think they would suit. In fact, I believe it will be good for him to interact with her. Kala will show him a thing or two as well." And with that, Boss left him. When the two women appeared in the room again with Kala, he smiled at her. She looked very frustrated.

"I'm supposed to hire these two women." Riss told her that Boss had thought it a good idea and why. "Oh. I guess that makes some sense. I might need the extra hands."

Riss laughed, thinking if there was any one more capable of holding a child, it was his wife. He couldn't wait to tell her so.

While she ate her dinner, he told her everything that was going to happen and also shared the book with her. As soon as she looked at him after touching it, he could see the million and one questions start to form in her mind. Smiling, he told her to wait until they were working and most of her questions would be answered.

"The cook, he's staying?" Riss nodded. "Good. I think I'd love being able to eat like this every day. Lily said we'd never gain a pound either."

"You will now, but that's to be expected." When she smiled at him, he knew something was up. "What's going on, Kala? What do you keep from me?"

"Oh, I'm going to keep a lot from you for the next few months. I think I want to see your face when all this comes to pass." Riss started to look at what she knew, but she put up her hand. "I'm your wife and you love me, right?"

"Of course I do. Why would you ask such a thing?" She kissed him as she ate the last slice of pie, giving him only one bite of it.

"Good. Then I'd very much like for you to stay away from any locked places you see in my head. If you really want to know, I can't stop you, but I'd very much like to have something I can surprise you with."

Riss nodded. He wasn't sure, but he thought she was enjoying this too much. After her dinner, they walked through the house to see what else they may need to fill it. Their home was wonderful.

Chapter 14

Michael looked over his list and leaned back in his chair. Things were moving along nicely for now, and he had to smile. In just over a year he'd have his men just where he wanted them. And all of them would be the better for it. Especially Tholan.

Tholan would be the hardest to bring to this. He'd been so upset all those decades ago when he'd caused his charge so much harm. She'd long since died, but Tholan still kept the pain of it in his heart. And Michael was afraid that it was what kept Tholan from being the kind of man they all knew he could be.

The woman that they'd picked for him was going to not just shock the man, but he'd be harder to convince that she was meant for him. She was the descendant of his charge, a woman, who, much like her ancestor, was hard to make stay still.

"Do you think he will hate me for a time?" Michael looked at Boss as He sat in the chair across from him. "I know that you think it wrong, but she will be the best thing for him."

"Tholan will be upset, but I do not think he will hate you for it. Especially when he falls in love." Boss nodded. "When do you want them to be introduced? Soon?"

Boss looked around the large office and at the pictures of the woman with their protectors. They were in no kind of order, just their pictures. And beneath those were pictures of the protectors that would come to them.

"You have them in a good order. Agon will come next. Then Galin." Boss looked at him. "Galin will be hard. Someone will need to understand his humor. Do you think she will?"

"Yes. There are times that I've visited her that I thought that she and he will not suit. But that is the point, is it not?" Boss nodded and then got up to stand in front of the wall of pictures.

"After Galin, then I think Arryn. After him, Valyn." Boss changed the two pictures that were not in the order He said and looked at Tholan's. "He will be last. It will be good for him to think he is not into this scheme of ours. I think when his time comes, Tholan will not thank us at first but try to deny it harder than anyone. I think I will enjoy that most."

"Tholan will need to make some changes soon so that he is in the rotation." Boss nodded and sat back down. "Who do you want to take his job when we send him to earth again?"

Boss laughed, and Michael was nervous. Whoever it was He had in mind wasn't going to be someone that Michael would like, he just knew it. And when He told him, Michael groaned.

"You cannot be serious. Him? You would have him work on the rotation and the schedule? I don't think you've thought this through."

"Oh, but I have. And he will be perfect. Tholan will be so frustrated when he trains him he might welcome a wife from earth." Boss laughed again. "And how can he refuse me? I'm Boss."

Michael was sure that Tholan would have plenty to say, but he doubted very much he'd come to Boss about it. Michael could see a long road ahead of him when the time came. Yes, sir, a very hard road indeed.

About the Author

Kathi Barton, author of the bestselling series Force of Nature, lives in Nashport, Ohio with her husband Paul. In addition to writing full time Kathi likes to spend time with her eight grandkids, three children and three children-in-laws. She writes to relax and have fun.

Her muse, a cross between Jimmy Stewart and Hugh Jackman brings them to life for her readers in a way that has them coming back time and again for more. Her favorite genre is paranormal romance with a great deal of spice. You can visit Kathi on line and drop her an email if you'd like. She loves hearing from her fans. aaronskiss@gmail.com.

Follow Kathi on her blog:
http://kathisbartonauthor.blogspot.com/